THE BEGINNING OF THE WORLD
IN THE MIDDLE OF THE NIGHT

Stories of family and magic, lost souls and superstition.
Spirits in jam jars, mini-apocalypses,
animal hearts and side shows.
Mermaids are on display at the local aquarium.
A girl runs a coffin hotel on a remote island.
A boy is worried his sister has two souls.
And a couple are rewriting the history of the world.

'Interwoven with myth and fairy tale, these stories are
surprising, delightful, by turns dangerous and joyful, like
walking through a mirror and discovering a world that you
both recognise and have never seen before.'

Rachel Joyce

'This book is full of character and magic,
and I found myself mesmerised.'

Claire Fuller

'These stories are weaved together like silvery
fishing nets. Like shimmering, jewel-bright worlds.'

Helen McClory

'Oh my good god. What a book! It's so STRANGE and magical and the writing is just beautiful. I loved it. I was hooked from the first sentence. A genuine pleasure to read.'
Louise O'Neill

'Enchanting and whimsical, curiously beautiful and illuminating.'
Carys Bray

'Intimate, fantastical and true, like all great fairytales, Campbell's stories hold whole worlds in single sentences.'
Kiran Millwood Hargrave

'Magical, dark and dreamy. The best short story collection I've read this year.'
Kirsty Logan

THE BEGINNING OF THE WORLD IN THE MIDDLE OF THE NIGHT

Also by Jen Campbell

NON-FICTION
Weird Things Customers Say in Bookshops
More Weird Things Customers Say in Bookshops
The Bookshop Book

POETRY
The Hungry Ghost Festival

CHILDREN'S BOOKS
Franklin's Flying Bookshop

THE BEGINNING
OF THE WORLD
IN THE MIDDLE
OF THE NIGHT

JEN CAMPBELL

TWO
ROADS

www.tworoadsbooks.com

First published in Great Britain in 2017 by Two Roads
An imprint of John Murray Press
An Hachette UK company

3

A CIP catalogue record for this title is available from the British Library

Hardback ISBN 978 1 473 65353 5
Ebook ISBN 978 1 473 65354 2

Typeset by Palimpsest Book Production Ltd, Falkirk, Stirlingshire

Printed and bound by Clays Ltd, St Ives plc

Hodder & Stoughton policy is to use papers that are natural,
renewable and recyclable products and made from wood grown in sustainable
forests. The logging and manufacturing processes are expected to conform
to the environmental regulations of the country of origin.

Hodder & Stoughton Ltd
Carmelite House
50 Victoria Embankment
London EC4Y 0DZ

www.hodder.co.uk

Contents

'It is true, we shall be monsters, cut off from all the world; but on that account we shall be more attached to one another.'

Mary Shelley, *Frankenstein*

The Beginning of the World
in the Middle of the Night

Animals

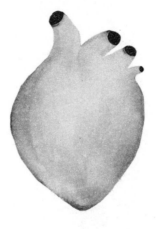

These days, you can find anything you need at the click of a button.

That's why I bought her heart online.

It was delivered this morning along with my groceries, tucked inside a cardboard box, red oozing out the sides. They'd tied a half-hearted bow around the edges, a tag with promises of customer satisfaction and a thirty-day warranty.

'Our hearts are played classical music from the moment they begin to grow.
Bred to love. Built to last.'

It is crimson.

I lift it out and the heart spreads itself across my palm like an octopus. I tickle one of its valves and it flops down onto the kitchen counter, panicking. I pick it up again. I've heard other men talk of fishing and hauling. Of holding gasping flounder in their fists that they then throw on an open fire.

Perhaps this is it.

The heart flutters.

There isn't anything quite like holding love in your bare hands.

I read the blood-soaked leaflet stuck to the bottom of the box.

This heart is from a swan.

Good. They say birds are easy to tame.

'There, there, little one,' I say. 'It's going to be OK.'

I stroke it gently with one finger and whistle birdsong.

It visibly calms.

First things first. You need to treat hearts the same way you treat pets, that's something my mother understood just fine. You shower hearts profusely and then stop. The stopping is important. You have to wait for the heart to become desperate; wait for it to think you've forgotten all about it. Then – and only then – do you smother it again with love and affection.

It's the only way.

It's how hearts grow.

It's how they learn to never leave your side.

Hearts also need good nutrition and plenty of exercise. If you purchase one, make sure you keep it hydrated. If you're new to this, you need to buy yourself a heart case until you decide whether or not this is The One. Hearts come in all different shapes and sizes, of course, but they don't need bespoke sleeping quarters. Just somewhere warm and damp, close to human skin. My mother said, correctly, that love can fill any room.

I'd recommend keeping your heart case strapped to your chest under your clothes to stop dogs chasing you down the street. Make sure you buy your heart from a reputable source, too. I once bought a faulty one that took on a will of its own and tried to bury its way under my skin. I'd never felt pain like it. That was the last time I took a seller recommendation from my next-door neighbour. Mind you, he's been using glass hearts for the best part of a year, now, and neither he nor his partner look happy about it. More fool them.

I slide the swan heart into my heart case and hide it under my jumper, feeling the pulse of both my heart and the swan heart, slightly out of sync. Love needs to be trained in warmth and rhythm and reliability. Don't let anyone tell you otherwise.

I rinse out the box the heart came in. Cora always likes to say I use too much washing-up liquid but there's no crime in wanting things clean. I slot the box into the recycling. Recycling is important. You shouldn't litter the world.

That's why I've kept her.

Most of her, anyway.

*

I check on Cora, and go into my study to Google 'swan'.

The Celtic goddess of sleep transforms into a swan every other year.

There are seven types of swan, including mute swans and tundra swans.

Swans aggressively protect their nests.

Swans mate for life.

Swan meat was a delicacy during the reign of Elizabeth I, reserved for the wealthy and noble.

The word 'swan' comes from the Indo-European root 'swen', which means to sound, to sing.

I do like it when Cora sings.

I put on my shoes to head to the park. On the way out, I spy Thomas watering his garden. He's humming a tune I'm not familiar with and stands in a sea of blue forget-me-nots. He raises his hand in an effort at *hello*, but he's looking elsewhere. I raise a hand back, just in case he sees, and stride away.

Many hundreds of years ago, a poet was walking along the Boyne river in Ireland, and saw a flock of swans flying high above him. He picked up a stone and threw it in their direction and one of the swans tumbled out of the sky. The poet ran to catch it and saw that it was no longer a swan but a woman. Her arm was broken and she looked up at him, wildly, and said: 'Thank you. Demons came to my deathbed and turned me into a bird. I have been trapped ever since and flying for so long, I didn't know if it would ever end.' The poet held her close, then took her home, and her heart was thumping, thumping, thumping.

The number 81 bus is a hive of misery.

The woman sitting next to me is attached to a portable oxygen machine. She tries to hide it under a blanket, but it's not something you can easily conceal. She's been sitting down for at least four stops, but I can still hear her breath rattling. She constantly checks her pulse. Every so often she heaves as though her organs are trying to propel themselves out into the world. I grimace. We all do. Stupid woman. I can almost smell the meat rotting away inside her. We turn our heads to the window in unison and pretend she doesn't exist.

I do a gentle lap around the pond when I arrive at the park. My resting heart rate is approximately fifty beats per minute. This is impressive, of course, but I try not to tell too many people (though inevitably it slips into conversations). I don't want to make others feel bad about themselves.

I try to focus on my breathing as I jog. I think of two swans and their necks meeting to form the shape of a heart. I think of *Swan Lake* and mistaken identities. I think of Zeus, tumbling down to earth to cause chaos as a god hidden in a swan's body, and I yell as a flyaway football narrowly misses the side of my chest. I cross my arms, and continue running, blood pounding in my ears and the swan heart beating so furiously it sounds like it's trying to take off.

At the far end of the park, there is a bandstand. People are clustered around a brass quartet, who are blue in the face, and a man in a ridiculous heart costume. He dances on the spot, both to keep warm and to draw attention to the moneybox he is shaking in people's faces: 'All proceeds go to the British Love Foundation! Please give generously!'

Give me strength. I dodge the crowd and, finally, find what I've been looking for. A young boy and his mother are feeding the ducks, and next to those squabbling ducks is a swan. Huge, white, majestic. The swan heart strains to the edge of its case at the sound of water and other birds. There are many people milling around. This might cause a scene. Then again, they do say that love loves an audience. So, I pick up a stone from the side of the path, take careful aim, and fling.

The young boy screams and someone drops their tuba.

Most people pretend not to notice the dead swan draped over my shoulders as I walk back home. They part to let me through, some tutting as they do so. The swan is heavier than it looks, and its wings keep trailing along the ground, tripping me up. I hoist it higher. Its neck dangles down, beak bouncing off the case of the swan heart beneath, which is practically chirruping. The bus driver refused to let me on, miserable bastard, but the exercise will do me good. I'm sweating, in spite of the wind.

Thomas is still watering his garden when I get home. There are pools forming around his ankles.

'Hey,' he says, waving with the wrong hand so the sprinkler he's holding dowses his clothes. 'Oh! Nice swan.'

'Thanks,' I say.

'Is it all right? It looks a bit . . . floppy.'

'It's dead.'

'Oh!' He shudders. 'Doesn't the Queen own all the swans in the country, or something?'

I fumble for my keys. 'Bye, Thomas.'

'Oh, OK. Bye.'

I slam the door behind me and let the swan tumble to the floor. It stares up at me, blankly. He's right, though, Thomas. The Queen technically does own all unmarked swans in open water. Not that she'd ever exercise her rights. They don't make queens like they used to

There was a time when jealous queens ate the hearts of their daughters. Elisabeth of Austria, a real-life nineteenth-century princess, used to sleep with raw meat on her face, to keep her skin young and freckle-free. She had hair that took hours to brush, and she would wash it with egg yolk and brandy. At the age of sixty, she was stabbed through the heart by an anarchist who thought she looked ugly. Her corset was so tight that she didn't die for several hours. Her heart bled out slowly, twitching in a cage.

Birds and hearts are similar in so many ways, you see. I nudge the dead swan with my foot.

It's like poetry, really.

I check on Cora, who hasn't moved, and drag the bird into the kitchen. It takes an age to pluck, as I try to keep the feathers whole. I'll get Cora to make a skirt with them, one that sweeps the floor. She can wear it along with her bearskin coat and wolf-tooth crown, and I'll take her dancing. The white feathers gleaming against her dark skin, the two of us never breaking eye contact so everyone else feels uncomfortable. We can arch our necks and point our feet. Parade across the floor.

Swans were sacred to Druids, who thought they repre-sented the soul. They believed these birds could travel between our world and the world of the dead, and, because storytellers brought news from all worlds, they were given ceremonial cloaks called *tuigen*, made out of songbird feathers. The hoods of these cloaks were decorated with the feathers of a swan.

Cora loves stories; she deserves a cloak of feathers.

I take off my jumper, and unstrap the heart case under-neath. I don't want to distress my newly bought heart by keeping it on me as I dissect my kill. I can almost hear it resisting as I put it down, away from the warmth of my body. It shudders slightly. It misses me. Good.

I pull on an apron and close the blinds.

I sharpen my knives.

Butchery is an art form lost on many.

The six o'clock news filters out from the radio.

Today's headlines: US scientists remain sceptical of North Korea's claims it has created the Elixir of Love. A video from a woman in northern England has gone viral, in which she says she is willing to donate her heart to save someone else's relationship. The suicidal forty-two-year-old from Northumberland is currently accepting couples' CVs via email, so she can pick one to donate her heart to.

I slice through the breast meat.

The Aphrodite Heart Factory in east London has seen a record number of animal rights protestors, after its announcement that it will be opening five new branches just north of the city. The activists, who have all rejected animal heart transplants, choosing instead to suffer with heart disease, petition for the abolition of the animal heart market. The Prime

Minister calls for calm, insisting that these new facto-
ries are simply a precautionary measure, not a sign
that love levels are plummeting to an all-time low.
   He released this statement earlier this afternoon.
'Whilst we continue to manufacture hearts for our
own needs, we must also take great care to cater for
others, by sending out hearts and doctors to those
suffering in foreign lands. Love translates into all
languages, and should know no bounds.'

I locate the swan's wishbone and put it to one side for
later, then I pull the swan heart out from its ribcage, blood
congealing on my fingertips.

   It's a special moment.

   It's still warm.

   I lick my lips.

   It's not unusual to eat animal hearts. Dare I say it's not
unusual to eat human hearts, either. There are odd people
out there who place adverts looking for strangers to eat
their hearts while they struggle to stay alive, which is hardly
arousing, but the actual act of eating human hearts goes
back centuries, probably millennia. One eccentric in the
1800s, William Buckland, used to eat all manner of strange
things. Bluebottles and toasted mice, panthers and puppies.
At least I don't do that. Mind you, William did also eat
the heart of Louis XIV, which had been embalmed for a

hundred and fifty years. He simply grabbed the silver container on display at dinner, ripped out the contents and swallowed it whole. That's not something I'd recommend. Hearts should be fresh. Still beating, if at all possible.

I trim the fat from the edges of the swan heart and begin working on a marinade. My favourite is a simple one. Two tablespoons of olive oil, one of sherry vinegar, a splash of Worcestershire sauce, a pinch of salt, oregano and black pepper. I chop the heart finely and line it in the marinade. It'll need to sit for an hour or so. Enough time to clean up, freeze the carcass, make a side salad and check on everything downstairs.

The swan heart I bought online still sits on the counter top. It's beating slower than before. Every so often, it jumps in its case, trying to get my attention. I wonder if it's concerned I'm about to cut it into tiny pieces, too. Part of me feels sorry for it, like a fool. I make soothing noises and reattach it to my chest. The heart sighs with relief. We're bonding. Once I've cooked and eaten tonight's meal, we'll bond further. Independent studies have shown that if a human consumes a heart from the same species intended to be put inside his or her lover, then there is a greater chance of creating a lifetime bond. Love consumes you, so you must consume it.

I carry the chopping board to the sink, squeeze in a good amount of washing-up liquid and relish the silence where a reprimand would be. Through the kitchen blinds, suds up to my elbows, I spy Thomas and James in their living room. They're sitting side by side on their new designer sofa. No doubt they deliberately left their curtains open so the world could see. A poster image for a glass heart relationship. Like a bloody art installation.

The water's a murky red, so I drain it and refill.

Thomas and James appear to be watching television, though their expressions give nothing away. They were far more interesting when they argued and fought and cared about each other. I'll never understand glass hearts. Glass may be recyclable but it's also cold and weak. Amorphous, with no clear shape or form. Charles VI of France believed he was made of glass. He carried pieces of iron in his clothing to protect himself from breaking. Fragile and precious, he was called Charles the Mad and Charles the Well-Beloved. That's not the kind of love I want, even if it does sit on a designer sofa.

I look around me. The kitchen floor is covered with feathers. There's a bloody handprint on the freezer door.

You can't say that's not exciting.

I grab the disinfectant.

It's dark outside and every house on the street is glowing like a planet. Every house, that is, apart from the Drurys' at number 143. Their semi-detached is a black hole. I'm not one for gossip but last month I heard they'd opted for a joint heart replacement, after it emerged that Mrs Drury had been somewhat unfaithful. They thought it would be romantic to go under the knife together, and wake up with two new hearts. French Angelfish hearts, to be precise. They'd picked them out together, genetically modified to beat as one. I gather a fistful of feathers. Love doesn't work like that. Love needs the dominant one to take the lead. Couples have tried to have their hearts replaced simultaneously before, even lying side by side on an operating table, falling asleep while holding hands, but they've all woken up and looked at each other and not known who it is they are looking at. Their hearts simply not in it anymore. I haven't seen the Drurys in weeks, though I spied their daughter packing her car with suitcases at the crack of dawn on Tuesday. She's one of those awful New Age newbie arseholes who have made a pact to focus on their own well-being. To never settle down with anyone, lest they get their hearts smashed to pieces. They blame the older generations for turning the world into a loveless place. They say they can make it on their own, that they don't need other halves. They wear badges that say things like 'No Love, No Problems.'

As though life can be that simple.

Not that it's safe having a youthful, perfect heart, anyway. Wandering the streets all shiny and new. We've all heard the rumours about small, remote villages that have been ransacked overnight by groups of expert thieves. Whole pockets of civilisation that have had their hearts wrenched out of their chests to sell on the black market. Some say that these villagers keep on living. Wandering, listless. Unable to love. Unable to die. Homes of heartless quiet. The closest we get here is jealous lovers turning to murder. But that's nothing new. Then there are the swingers: couples who want to swap hearts with other couples. Just for fun. But why bother to go out and find someone else, when you can mould what you already have?

I hang up my rubber gloves and stroke the heart case.

The swan heart purrs.

Cora's still sleeping in the next room. Her head wound is healing nicely, her chest a gaping hole with a pump firmly attached. I still need to unpack her open suitcase, though most of the garments are strewn across the carpet like human feathers. Like the times we'd hastily undress and fling our clothes across the floor.

What animals we were back then. Biting each other's lips. How vicious. How unpredictable.

I inject Cora with a fresh dose of anaesthetic, tuck her in, kiss her forehead, and tell her another story.

Once upon a time, a girl's father married a witch.

The witch turned her six brothers into swans, and they flew away.

Worried she would also be turned into a swan, the young girl packed her suitcase and hid in the deep forest, where the sunlight rarely visited, and there were many eyes looking out at her from the bodies of trees.

There, one of the swan brothers found her. Flapping his wings, he told his sister that she had the power to save them because her heart was so good. He said, if she sewed six tunics made of flowers, they would put them on and turn back into humans. He said it was a secret spell, and she wasn't allowed to talk to anyone until the tunics were finished. He said, if she did, the spell wouldn't work.

So the girl collected as many flowers as she could and began to sew.

She sewed sitting in a tree so the wolves couldn't get her.

But the world is a dark place, full of many kinds of wolves.

A group of men, out hunting, found the strange girl sewing flowers and asked her what she was doing. She couldn't speak, so she smiled, but that wasn't enough. She threw them her bracelet, which they caught, but that wasn't enough either. So, she took off her clothes and dropped them to the floor, in the hope they would see her good heart shining out of her chest.

Then they smiled back, and climbed up the tree, and decided to take her home.

She was taken to the young king of a neighbouring realm.

He looked at this silent girl with her good heart, and bought her immediately.

She married him without speaking a word.

The king's mother was angry about the marriage, because no woman was good enough for her only son.

For the next few years, this new queen continued to sew flower tunics without speaking. But the task was taking a long time because her mother-in-law destroyed every tunic out of spite, and she could only sew during the spring and summer months, for during the autumn all the flowers died.

'That silent girl is full of secrets,' the mother-in-law muttered. 'My heart is stronger than hers will ever be.'

When the silent queen gave birth to a child, the mother-in-law stole it and ordered that it be killed and baked in a pie. She smeared blood on the queen's mouth and told her son that his bride had eaten their daughter.

'Did you do it?' he asked his wife.

She shook her head but said nothing.

Crying, she went back to sewing tunics made of flowers, and the mother-in-law kept burning them, one by one.

When the silent queen gave birth to her second child, the same thing happened. The mother-in-law smeared blood across the queen's mouth and ordered the baby be killed.

'Did you do it?' the king asked.

The queen shook her head but said nothing at all.

'Her silent heart is a trap,' the king's mother whispered to her son. 'My heart is better. Time to burn her so she finds her words. Time to burn her until she shouts and screams.'

The morning the queen was to be burned, she walked down to the courtyard. She'd been up all night sewing as fast as she could for, several weeks earlier, she'd found a secret place to hide the tunics. This time they hadn't been destroyed, and now she had enough. She carried five tunics made of flowers and a sixth nearly complete but with one sleeve missing. As the fire was lit, she threw the tunics into the air and six swans appeared on the horizon. They swooped down and pulled on the tunics and immediately turned back into her brothers. The sixth still had a swan arm attached to his human body, which he flexed and admired in the light of the sun.

With the spell broken, the mute queen was able to speak. She told her husband how his mother had murdered their children. How she'd chopped them into pieces and baked them into pies. The king clasped his chest and declared his mother a witch. They tied her to a tree and burned her at the stake. Her skin melted in the heat, and her blood began to boil but her heart was so cold that the fire couldn't touch it.

The king pulled his mother's heart from the flames and put it in a jar.

He placed it on the mantelpiece where it shone blue in the dark.

Then the swan boys danced, and the silent girl sang, and the king wondered at the strangeness of the world.

I keep Cora's hearts in the basement.

They hang, suspended, in vases of alcohol.

Her original heart is on the far left, vaguely purple.

Then the wolf heart, glistening silver.

The deer heart, turning blue.

The fox heart, shrinking slowly.

And her most recent, the bear heart, growling quietly to itself.

Is it terribly clichéd to think of this as a room filled with love? Failed love, obviously, but love nevertheless. I like to come here when I need reminding that everything can be fixed. That the world just needs medicine, and people can change. People do change. I've seen it. I've made it happen.

It's not unusual to keep hearts. Royals once demanded their hearts be buried apart from their bodies, and butchers and cooks were hired to cut them free. When Henry I died in Normandy after eating poisonous eels, his heart was sewn into the hide of a bull and taken back to England. The rest of him was left in France to rot under the ground.

Home is where the heart is.

I found Cora ten years ago. We both had articles published in the same journal. Hers was on the history of fairy tales, mine on the poetry of the Romantics. In my essay, I'd touched on the death of Percy Shelley. How, when he was cremated, his friend Edward Trelawny had reached in and pulled his heart out from the flames. His wife, Mary Shelley, took him to court and fought hard to get the heart back. She won and she kept it in her writing desk until the day she died.

And people wonder where *Frankenstein* comes from.

That evening, as Cora listened to me, not saying a word, I could see her good heart shining out through her chest. Thundering and garbling like some underwater train. Vines sneaking up to block out the world and her homemade floral dress glowing amber in the dark.

In the Middle Ages, people believed that a heart contained a person's soul. That all of their beliefs, thoughts, feelings and memories lived inside there, as though written inside a book. God was thought to have a copy of every-one's hearts, with records of how good or bad they were scribbled inside. Sometimes, he would write on these records, and this writing would transmit to the replicas in human bodies on earth. There are legends of saints who were said to have images drawn on their organs by divine power. Touched by the hand of God.

So, when we say we are 'turning over a new leaf', we

are referring to the book of our heart. It means we are starting over. Making fresh starts. New hearts.

This swan heart will be Cora's fifth heart in ten years.

Her fourth in the last two.

The fox heart made her nocturnal.

The deer heart made her flee.

The bear heart made her possessive.

The wolf heart gave her rage.

The swan heart clamours in its case.

I head back upstairs. The house feels like it's breathing. This is home. This is home. This is home.

My mother's heart sits on the mantelpiece. Baby blue, encased in glass.

Next to it, my wedding present to Cora. A replica of a French tapestry from 1400, called 'The Offering of the Heart'. It shows a man giving his pulsing heart to a woman as a symbol of his devotion.

Love as an art form.

In 1956, Erich Fromm wrote a book called *The Art of Loving*. In it, he argued that the active character of true love requires four basic elements: care, responsibility, respect and knowledge.

*Love is a decision, it is a judgment, it is a promise.
If love were only a feeling, there would be no basis
for the promise to love each other forever . . . Love
isn't something natural . . . It isn't a feeling, it is a
practice.*

Cora said my mother loved me an unhealthy amount.
Whilst the world was running out of love, my mother was
trying to hoard it. She clung to me so desperately, Cora
deemed it unnatural. For that is what love is. She told me
I'd better deal with it or else she'd leave forever.

So I did.

I admit it felt strange, holding a pillow over my mother's
face like that. How, when I carved her open to extract her
overflowing heart, her body was still twitching. How I used
five bottles of washing-up liquid to get the blood off the
kitchen floor. How I burned her body in the back yard,
and sprinkled her ashes on the orange trees.

When I came home, carrying my mother's heart, Cora
screamed.

She claimed she'd never meant for me to go that far.

She yelled she'd only meant that I should talk to her.

She cried that just the thought of what I'd done made
her sick.

That's the first time she tried to leave.

Despite Cora's protests, all her academic research into fairy tales had shown that, for love to flourish, parents needed to die. And as I grabbed her by the wrist and dragged her back inside the house, I reminded her of that very fact and spat: 'Aren't all of us just trying to find our happily ever after?'

Hundreds of years ago, when French kings and queens died, their hearts were mummified in silver urns and hidden in various cathedrals across the city of Paris. During the French Revolution, these were stolen by revolutionaries, and some hearts were sold in secret to artists. They liquidised them, mixed them with myrrh and created a highly sought-after paint called 'mummy brown'.

They say a mother's love is truly unconditional.

If these factory-created animal hearts keep failing, perhaps I can put my mother's heart inside Cora.

Perhaps that is the answer.

I take the swan heart out of its case and place it on top of Cora's cold skin.

It twitches, as though trying to get back to me.

It's wondering where I am.

Hearts are babies. Beating, blind, vulnerable babies.

I scoop the heart back up and it shudders with pleasure. I throw it from palm to palm and watch it switch between panic and joy. Then I stroke it, and hold it close, and it curls up to go to sleep.

When this heart cannot survive without me, when it consistently whimpers and diminishes if away from my side, that is when I will place it inside Cora.

And Cora will come back to me, wide-eyed and so deeply in love that she won't know how to function properly. She'll need me. Really, truly need me. No shouting, no packing her bags, no trying to run away from a man she says she can no longer stand.

She will love me.

I will make her love me.

The timer in the kitchen pings.

Long ago, there was a giant in Norway who kept his heart outside of his body so that he could live forever. But keeping his heart somewhere else had its down side, too. He turned men to stone in rage, for they could love and he could not, and he locked a princess inside his house to stop her marrying the sons of kings.

One day, a prince, whose six brothers had already been turned to stone by the giant, entered the giant's house and found the princess there. She told him they would have to find the giant's heart and destroy it so she could be released. The giant said it was buried under the floor, but that was a lie. He said it was in the cupboard, but that was a lie, too. Finally, the giant laughed and said he kept his heart on a faraway island, inside a warm egg, in the nest of a swan.

The prince went in search of this faraway island, and at last found the giant's heart, inside an egg, in the nest of a swan. He squeezed the egg and the giant cried out in pain, clutching his chest. He sank to his knees and asked for forgiveness. The prince gleefully demanded he release all his stone victims and the princess, first. The giant did so, so scared was he for the fate of his heart. The men became human, the princess was free, and the giant wept, believing he was saved.

But then the prince smirked and crushed the giant's heart anyway. Because hearts are meant to be crushed, and you cannot hide them anywhere for love, nor money. Especially not love.

I stroke Cora's cheek, her new heart dripping in my hand.

The prince married the princess, and they loved each other. Until the love ran out.

Then they fought, and they cried and they filled themselves with hatred.

Thank goodness we no longer live in a world like that.

Jacob

Dear Miss Winter,

My name is Jacob Quinn.

If I am home from school in time, I watch you do the weather forecast on the six o'clock news. Most of the time you predict the weather correctly. My mum says that the world is an unpredictable place, so you must be very good at your job. Well done. I hope they pay you well.

I also hope you don't mind me writing to you. This letter is not about the weather (sorry), but you seem like a very friendly person and I have some questions I need to ask. There are two reasons I think you might be good at answering these questions. 1. Because you are good at understanding the weather and so I think you might be good at understanding people. And 2. because of your name (more on that later, please keep reading).

I am writing to you about my sister. She is called Catherine and she does philosophy at university. She moved out last year but still visits during the holidays.

When she comes home, she spends a lot of her time asking questions when people ask her things. Dad calls this answering back, but Cath says we shouldn't blindly accept things. She says that if our answers aren't questions then we're not thinking hard enough and we're not pushing ourselves to our limits. But she also says that limits don't exist so I'm not really sure what she's looking for. It's like going to the corner shop to buy some Smarties, then picking them out of the packet one by one, hoping to find a silver one. It's like Cath knows there isn't going to be a silver Smartie but she's still asking 'where is it?' and 'can it exist?' and telling us we should be asking those questions, too. I don't know. I don't really understand philosophy. My dad calls it stupid, which is one of the reasons I am writing this letter to you and not to him.

Anyway. I am sidetracking. Cath's point was that questions are good things. Like water, and the colour yellow, and strawberry fruit gums. Cath says that questions make us expand as people, which makes me think we're all like elastic bands, and that does something funny to my stomach.

Something else that does funny things to my stomach is that Cath is changing and I am worried about her. She says I shouldn't call her Cath any more, because that isn't her name. She decided to change it, so that she could be someone new. She went down to the council (which is where we send money so that the country works properly) and she signed her name away and put it in a drawer along with her baby teeth.

Now, she's called Anna.

Like that old film *Anna and the King*. There was also a person in the Bible called Anna who prophesied about Jesus. Cath-Anna says that didn't have anything to do with her decision-making, because she isn't religious. She just likes the name. There's a girl in my class at school called Anna. I asked her if she knew that Anna was a lady in the Bible but she shook her head and told me she's Jewish and she didn't think it was the same. Names are strange things, Miss Winter, sharing them doesn't make you the same at all. I find this odd when I think about it hard. Maybe we should all have numbers instead because Mum says that those are infinite.

Over Christmas, I went into Cath-Anna's bedroom to tell her that dinner was ready, and I found all of her old exercise books from school spread out across the floor. She'd pulled them out from the cupboard. A long time ago, Cath-Anna and I covered our school books in wallpaper that we got from a shop, so that they would look more interesting. When we were in the shop, we had to pretend that we were decorating the living room and needed wallpaper samples. Mum called this a white lie. (Why do lies have colours?) But when I went into Cath-Anna's room, all of her books were on the floor and she'd crossed out 'Cath' on every single one. It was as if she didn't want to exist any more. That did something funny to my stomach, too.

My sister has been acting differently for quite a long time now, but Mum says we're not supposed to talk about it. I said this to Cath-Anna and she rolled her eyes and said that not talking about things is bad. She said that silence is suffocating, like being in a box. Then she told me about a cat in a box who can exist and not exist at the same time. She went on about this for a long time, then asked me if I understood. There are two things I don't understand about this, Miss Winter: 1. Why is a cat in a box in the first place? This is a very cruel thing to do. 2. Where is the cat going? If he is in a box, is his owner moving house or something, and how long will it take to drive there (because there is only so much air in one box)? But when I said these things to Cath-Anna, she giggled and rolled her eyes, even though my answers were questions and that's what she said all answers should be. Sometimes I think it is better to just let her talk about the cat in the box, even when I don't understand, because she seems happier that way. Perhaps that's fair.

Cath-Anna likes balance and justice and fairness. But she says that things don't always work out like that, and that's why we have to work hard to change things. She says making the world a better place is part of our job. But my main job is to go to school, and your job is to predict the weather, and Mum's job is in an office, though she had to stop that for a bit to do jury service. I thought Cath-Anna would be excited about Mum doing jury service because a courthouse is a place where they sort out balance and fairness. Mum said her case was a hung jury, though, which doesn't mean that they tried to kill themselves but that they couldn't think of an answer to whether the person was guilty or not. Mum said it was a shame, but that it was understandable because grown-ups don't know what they are doing most of the time. Is this true, Miss Winter? That sounds a bit scary.

As well as being worried about my sister, I am also worried about my mum. Cath-Anna and I have noticed that Mum buys flowers when she is stressed. She stands at the kitchen table and arranges them and then rearranges them so, if you come downstairs at nine o'clock at night and ask her where Dad is, you know that the answer will be one pink lily to the left, or one to the right, or a stalk snapped in two.

We have a lot of flowers in our house these days,

Miss Winter. Our kitchen looks like a garden. I decided to use these to draw pictures for my art homework. Taylor said I was gay for doing that and then he ripped up my picture and Miss Hudson got mad and gave him detention after school. Miss Hudson's our art teacher, and she has big red hair, which looks funny when she gets angry because it matches her red cheeks. Sometimes she gets really cross and goes through a door in the corner of the art room and doesn't come back for a while. We always thought it was a door to a staffroom, but one day a girl in our class opened it when Miss Hudson wasn't there and it turned out to be a cupboard. That means that Miss Hudson had been sitting in a cupboard all those times she'd been cross. Like that cat in a box. I understand why she did it, though. Sometimes having walls around you makes you feel safe. That's why I like the garden shed and our next-door neighbour's garage and hiding under my bed. Most people laughed when we found the cupboard but not Jewish Anna. She stamped her patent leather shoes and told Taylor to shut the hell up. Perhaps she likes small spaces, too.

Do you like small spaces, Miss Winter?

A few weeks ago, I had to think of something to do for my end of year art project. Miss Hudson said we had to draw or paint a picture based on the work of an artist we like. When she said this, I did what Cath-Anna told me to do, and replied with a question. I asked her why. She raised an eyebrow and said, 'Don't be silly, Jacob.' But I wasn't being silly.

We went to the art museum on a school trip to see some paintings and find inspiration. We had to go on the tube, which seemed to cause the teachers a lot of stress. Taylor was annoying because he kept trying to stop the doors closing at every station along the way. Taylor is an arsehole.

Some of the paintings at the museum are larger than the walls in our house. They had some sculptures, too. One was very rude. It was called *Humpty Fucking Dumpty*. Miss Hudson made us hurry past when she saw that and looked nervous. I think it was because there weren't any cupboards nearby.

We walked around the museum and looked at all the different art. There were a lot of naked people (in the paintings, not in the museum), and lots of portraits of kings and queens. My favourite picture was called *The Deluge*, which is the biggest painting I've ever seen. It was in a room called 'The Sublime in Crisis'. Cath-Anna says that the word Sublime means 'amazing' but that it can also mean other things, too. She says that it can be that feeling in the pit of your stomach when you stand on a high place and look around you, and you realise how big the universe is and how small you are in comparison to it. Perhaps you have this feeling, too, Miss Winter, when you fly in a helicopter to check on the weather in the sky.

The painting made me feel very small. Have you seen it? It's all waves and darkness. It shows the floods after Noah got away in the ark. I stood looking at the painting for ages, and then Jewish Anna came over and held my hand and looked at it with me, which made my stomach squirm. We didn't look at each other. We just stood there in silence, thinking about how big the world is. Then Taylor knocked over one of the sculptures and there was a big argument between Miss Hudson and one of the museum workers.

I really liked the painting, even though it made me feel tiny, and even though it was about something that happened in the Bible and I don't know if I believe in those things. I'm still interested in them though, because they are very dramatic, like *Coronation Street*, and also like the news. Sometimes you talk about floods on the news, Miss Winter. Floods like the one in this painting. Floods are scary things because we cannot control them, apart from trying to stop climate change. My grandma doesn't believe in climate change, though. She says we should pray for our souls, instead.

Sometimes I worry that my sister has two souls - one called Cath and one called Anna, and they're having a battle inside of her. But I don't know if this is scientifically possible. What do you think, Miss Winter? My sister says that she didn't want to be called Catherine, because it's a name my dad chose for her. She said that having that name made her feel lost at sea. She said she wanted to reinvent herself. She chose the name Anna because it is the same on both sides, and she likes balance. I asked Jewish Anna if she feels more balanced because of the way her name is written, instead of being called Catherine or something else. She thought hard about it and chewed on the end of her pencil, and then she said that she had never been called Catherine so she couldn't really tell, which is fair enough, even if it is a hung jury.

What about you, Miss Winter? Were you born with your last name, or did you change it because you thought it would be a good name to have for your job? If you didn't change it, do you think being born with it meant you were destined to talk about the weather? Is winter your favourite season? I would be very interested to know your thoughts on this. I don't know anyone else called Jacob, so I'm not really sure what my name means or whether I am destined to become something specific. I will have to wait and see.

For my art project, I decided to draw a flooded world. I used a mixture of pencils and oil paint and watercolour because I couldn't decide which one I liked best. I decided to put my sister in the painting. I put her right in the middle, lying on a raft on top of the waves. I only drew her as a stick person because I'm not very good at faces and because that way it was easy to make her look the same on both sides, like her new name.

Miss Hudson said that when we look at a painting, we are looking into our souls, and I hoped that when I looked at my painting, I would be able to look into my sister's soul (or two souls, if that's what she has) and finally understand who she is and why she's changed, and why she feels lost at sea.

But when I finished the painting and looked at it, I just saw the colour blue, and all the wobbly lines, and I didn't understand anything better. The reflection of the sky I drew in the water had stars in it, and these shone out like silver Smarties.

Yesterday, my mum told me that we are going to move into my aunt's house for a while. When I asked her why, she said it was a long story and she will tell me about it soon. She says Cath-Anna will come and visit us during the summer but my dad will be left behind.

I am excited to move but nervous, too. Where do you live, Miss Winter? My aunt's house is on top of a hill, and she has a cat. Once we move there, I will invite Jewish Anna round for tea and, if you say it isn't going to rain, we will draw pictures of the sky sitting in our new back garden.

At the moment, I am writing this to you lying under my bed. My mum is packing up cardboard boxes and I am eating strawberry fruit gums. I will put one inside the envelope in case you are hungry. Are you hungry?

I will also include my painting, as a present. I hope you like it. Please take good care of my floating sister. I love her very much.

The world is a strange place, isn't it, Miss Winter? I hope we get to enjoy it for a long, long time.

How are you today? Is the sun shining?

(I would say I am sorry for asking so many questions but I believe that questions are very important things.)

Yours sincerely,
Jacob Quinn

Plum Pie.
Zombie Green.
Yellow Bee.
Purple Monster.

When you grow up, who or what do you want to be?

Out on the road, Jack came across a man who said he'd buy his cow for a handful of magic beans. Five, to be precise. He said if Jack ran back home and buried them in his garden, a plant would grow there. A plant so tall it would make friends with the sky.

But what if Jack took those magic beans and planted them inside himself, instead?

Swallowed them down so they were hidden away inside him.

Growing, growing, *glowing*.

Poppy lies down and covers herself in green leaves.

'Am I alive or am I dead?' She giggles, trying not to move her mouth.

'You're both,' I say.

'Wrong! Wrong wrong wrong.'

She writhes on the ground like an animated rag doll. A sea of aquamarine.

Ivy's lounging in the tree house, wearing sunglasses shaped like clouds.

Madame Honey wanders between the tents, covered in bees, ticking things off on her clipboard. She pulls out a tape measure and lines it along the shoots poking out from Clover's torso. She scribbles down some numbers while Clover whistles, photosynthesising in the sun.

I count seeds in the palm of my hand.

One.

Two.

Tree.

OK, bad pun. Sorry.

This summer, when they collected us from the train station, Heath unfurled his hair, complete with twisting vines, and the buds swam along the path behind him like a bridal trail.

Jasmine used twenty face wipes to rid herself of the white paint clogging up her pores, and her green skin shone.

Daisy wouldn't stop talking until the sun went down, and the young nocturnal ones sleepily chased their shadows around the lawn.

'Welcome to this year's Camp.' Madame Honey's smile was sickly sweet. 'My, my, how big you've grown.'

On the first evening, we collected deadwood for a bonfire. We burned the coral petals Rose pulled from her mouth, presents from the plants growing quietly in her throat, and we told stories of our springs.

'I'm working at the greengrocer,' Heath told us. 'Trying to save up money for a trip.'

'Where to?'

'I want to find the umdhlebe.'

'The umdhlebe?'

'It's a poisonous tree that feeds on everything around it,' Heath said. 'It hasn't been seen in two hundred years but I bet I could find it.'

'Why would you want to find a poisonous tree?' Ivy snapped, hanging upside down from the tyre rope swing.

'Why not? I read a book that says botanists in South Africa found it, its soil fertilised by all the things it's killed.'

'Cheerful!'

'What will you do with it when you find it?'

Heath looked a little embarrassed. 'I don't know,' he shrugged. 'I guess I want to study it. See why it's feared. Perhaps sit with it for a while.'

Rose coughed and a tide of petals fell into the flames.

In the smoke, I saw a lonely tree, the ground around it littered with skeletons.

Lily didn't come back this year. No one got on at her stop.

We looked all over the train, including the dark, damp corners, where she sometimes liked to hide.

When we arrived, Madame Honey said: 'Lily's parents haven't returned our calls.'

And we all visibly wilted.

Lily was one of the best of us.

At the age of eleven, her hair turned white overnight and she started humming funeral songs.

That's the year they brought her here.

She always smelled of peppermint.

Last August, she swallowed apple seeds behind the shower block and didn't deny it when she was caught.

She was obsessed with HTML colour codes called hex triplets, and we rolled those across our tongues to try and taste the witchcraft. Soil up to our elbows, creating earth angels in the dust, listing our favourite colours.

They say that when you grow up you shouldn't have things like favourite colours because there are more important things in life. But that is bullshit. Lily and I had competitions, reciting shades off by heart:

Light Sea Green #20B2AA
Medium Orchid #BA55D3
Olive Drab #6B8E23
Thistle #D8BFD8
Seashell #FFF5EE
Burly Wood #DEB887
Tomato #FF6347
Ghost White #F8F8FF

Plum Pie. Zombie Green. Yellow Bee. Purple Monster.

We spat colours into the woods so the trees could swallow them.

We planned to paint the world.

And now we don't know where she's gone.

We look for her in the undergrowth, and down by the stream. We scan the newspaper she used to love, in case she's somehow made the headlines. While flicking through, the ink staining our fingertips, I remember the times we'd press flowers between the pages of a book of fables, trying to guess the type of tree it was made from. Pressing ourselves between the stories.

Ivy steals Madame Honey's mobile phone and we try to find Lily on the Internet, but we don't know her last name, and time and time again search engines simply show us the flowers she is named after.

But Lily isn't just a flower. Lily is our friend.

If Jack had taken those magic beans and planted them inside himself, he could have become one of us. He could have found himself in the headlines for different reasons, plastered to the side of Lily's tent, where she used to stick all the important news.

A doctor in Beijing has found a dandelion growing inside the ear canal of a sixteen-month-old girl. It had partially flowered, and was said to be very itchy.

A Russian man, suspected of having cancer, was found to have a small fir tree growing inside his left lung. When they took it out, he took it home.

These are our people.

Once, in Spain, a lily was found growing from the heart of a boy who couldn't read.

We have always tumbled out of newspapers and myth.

Hyacinths flowered from the blood of Apollo.

Carnations bloomed from the tears of Mary.

Snowdrops are said to be the hands of the dead.

You have to find us between the lines.

How strange they think we are.

Madame Honey passes out chalk, crayons and felt-tip pens.

'I want you all to sit and draw for thirty minutes,' she says.

'Draw what?' Clover scowls, her hair now peppered with flowers.

'Whatever comes to mind,' Madame Honey beams. 'No conferring.'

So, we pick up some colours and we all draw Lily.

Sleeping Lily.

Dancing Lily.

Shouting Lily.

Tiger Lily.

Lily climbing up a beanstalk, her hair blending with the clouds.

Lily locked up in a tower.

Lily talking with the trees.

Lily once told me that trees communicate underground. That they share food via symbiosis and don't tell humans that they're doing it.

'You just think you're looking at a forest, when you look at a forest,' Lily said. 'But that's not it, not really. The trees are talking. You can't see it, but they're talking. Forests aren't terrifying places. They just speak a different language.'

Forest Green #228B22

'Come on, Fern,' Jasmine nudges me. 'You're the storyteller. Where do you think Lily is?'

Well. Once upon a time, a king and queen were trying to have a baby. They tried for a long time, but each time the baby died. Then, many years later, the queen fell pregnant again. This time, she felt sure that things were different.

She craved food she'd never tasted before: pickled seaweed, sour radishes, honeycomb and even flowers. One of the flowers the queen loved to eat was called the Rampion Bellflower, also known as the Rapunzel. It didn't grow anywhere inside the palace grounds. It grew just beyond, in a secluded patch of earth, over the palace walls.

Every night, the queen begged the king to climb over the wall at the edge of the garden, to pick the Rapunzel flowers glowing under the moon. So he did. He carried them home piled on top of his crown. The queen chewed them as the sun rose, and brewed some petals in her tea.

One night, when the king was out collecting the flowers, a fairy appeared.

'Those are my flowers,' said the fairy.

'But I am the king,' said the king. 'And I own everything in this land. Besides, my pregnant wife craves them.'

'Then you may take the flowers but, in exchange, you must give me a gift.'

'What sort of gift?'

'You must give me your child.'

'Ha!' snorted the king. 'Come and collect her when she's born, if you think you're brave enough.'

So the fairy did. And the king discovered he was bound by magic to give her his child. The child was named Rapunzel, and the fairy locked her in a tower, for she was jealous of her hair. It grew long like vine and she braided it with bracken. She hung it out of the high windows for everyone to see. Her genes mixed with the flowers her mother had consumed. Part girl. Part plant. Raised up above the world . . .

'Are you saying that Lily has been stolen by a fairy?' Poppy asks, sipping Miracle-Gro.

'There's no such thing as fairies,' Ivy spits. 'Don't be stupid. The government's probably taken her away. I bet they've put her in isolation. For experiments.'

'We don't know that!'

'Oh, yeah? Well, where do you think she's gone then, huh? Where exactly did she go?'

'I don't know. Perhaps she ran away.'

Lily was not a wallflower.

I always thought of her as a waterwheel plant, a carnivorous green that could breathe underwater, propelled through the waves. A water lily. A plant like the Aldrovanda, which doesn't have roots. It's free-floating and traps whatever gets in its way, like a Venus Flytrap.

Lily was like that. Lily took no shit.

At the end of each summer, when the first leaves would fall, and they'd come at us with pliers for cuttings, Lily never went quietly.

'It's not OK, Fern,' she yelled, as they grabbed her by the wrists. 'It's not OK for them to do this. It's not OK, it's not OK, it's not OK.'

The first few weeks at Camp are always the easiest. We catch up, we let them measure us. We accept the Miracle-Gro and drink as much water as they put in front of us, and we let ourselves blossom in the sun. Here, we don't have to hide. No one's pointing at us in the street; no one's refusing to serve us at the supermarket. Here our differences can be prized, noticed and admired.

Ivy, all six foot seven of her.

Poppy and her hypnotic eyes.

Rose with her plants flowering in her throat.

Clover with her good luck vines sprouting out from her chest.

Jasmine with her sea-green skin that doesn't fade in winter.

And Heath, who embraces his pale-pink flowers. They go by the name of Erica. He calls them the other half of his soul.

But now the summer is ending, and the September wind is here.

'Lily used to think that we could cross-breed with other plants, if we swallowed certain seeds,' Poppy says. 'She said if we became more than one thing, it would make us even stronger.'

'What, cross-pollination?'

'Isn't that what they say about breeding dogs? Mongrels, and stuff?'

'You better not be calling me a dog.'

'Aren't we already cross-breeds?' Rose hiccoughs. 'I mean, we're already more than one thing.'

How to Cut a Rose for Winter

1. Begin pruning from the base.
2. Always prune dead wood back to healthy tissue.
3. Remove any weak branches.
4. Roses have a habit of spreading. Keep them under control.
5. Cuts must be clean, so keep your secateurs sharp.

When Madame Honey disappears, as she does at the end of every summer, and the tree surgeons take her place, with sharp tools and needles, feeding tubes and weed killer, we are ready.

When all is quiet and the moon is out, Ivy and Clover use their vines as extra limbs to prise open the doors of the laboratory, and we all race in. Daisy gasps. It's humid, with moisture clinging to the windows, and we see ourselves inside, lining the shelves. All the cuttings they've taken from us, growing up in glass cages. Parts of our bodies labelled. Sterile and dull.

We smash the glass.

We grab ourselves.

We run.

Oh, how we run.

Packets of seeds slide across the vinyl floor and jolt at every pot-hole.

'Tell us another story,' Heath pleads, as we pull out onto the motorway. Ivy bent over the wheel of our stolen van and us huddled in the back, our arms filled with green light.

OK. Once there was a creature called a *lilit*. *Lilits* appear across the world, ducking and diving through history and culture. But wherever they crop up, they are night spirits. Demons, whose souls are trapped in the abyss. Once, a god reached for a *lilit* and a woman called Lilith appeared. A witch, with a will of her own. But she didn't look the way men wanted her to look, and she didn't do the things they wanted her to do. So they cast her out into the night, where she bore children in the dark. Strange children. Fantastical children. Children with names pulled out from the soil.

Ivy revs the engine and the wind trickles in through the cracked windows of the van.

Plum Pie. Zombie Green. Yellow Bee. Purple Monster.

Every so often, we pull into fields and duck into forests, where we plant parts of our rescued selves.

They shiver pleasantly in the night-time air, surprised to find themselves in the wild.

'How long do you think it will be before they catch us?' Jasmine asks, peering out at the road behind us, where the sky is turning firebrick coral.

I shrug, hoping it's long enough to spread ourselves far and wide.

Out on the road, Jack came across a man who said he'd buy his cow for a handful of magic beans. Five, to be precise. He said if Jack ran back home and buried them in his garden, a plant would grow there. A plant so tall it would make friends with the sky.

But what if Jack took those magic beans and planted them inside himself, instead?

Swallowed them down so they were hidden away inside him.

Growing, growing, *glowing.*

Jasmine tears open packets of seeds and pours them into our waiting hands. We cup them like grains of sand. Tip them into our mouths and swallow.

*

At the next petrol station, I find a stamp crumpled at the bottom of my rucksack. We all scribble a letter on an empty packet of tulip seeds and address it to Lily's favourite newspaper. We want to place an advert, in the hope that she might see it. We argue over what it should say. I want to send her a secret message in HTML colour codes. #7D0541 #CFECEC, which means 'Bullet Shell' and 'Pale Blue Lily', to let her know that we are fighting and we hope she's fighting, too.

'She might see it and think we hope she's dead,' Ivy says. 'Bullet shell sounds aggressive.'

'What do you suggest, then?'

Rose raises a timid hand. 'Why don't we just list her favourite colours? To let her know she's on our mind?'

So that's what we do.

Our version of Morse code.

Lily, we love you. We hope that you are thriving. x
#7D0541
#54C571
#E9AB17
#461B7E

Plum Pie. Zombie Green. Yellow Bee. Purple Monster.

In the Dark

I was in the kitchen doing the dishes when he walked in. I don't know why I didn't tell him to get the hell out of my house. I don't know why my first question wasn't: 'Who are you?' It might have been because he looked so lost; I remember thinking that much. He looked severely out of place, walking in from the garden, as though he'd just found a whole new world. He looked apologetic about the whole thing, actually.

I didn't recognise his uniform, but I suppose I must have guessed he was a soldier, because I vaguely remember thinking: 'My God, what if he's got a gun?' But clearly I didn't panic about that, otherwise I probably would have run away or pushed him out the door. I think I would have done that, anyway. But then I suppose we never really know what we're going to do in these situations until we find ourselves doing it. Brains can rationalise a lot of strange things. Memories are complicated, too.

He said something but he didn't appear to say it to me. I thought perhaps he was speaking into a radio, one hidden out of sight. I couldn't understand what he was saying, or what language he was saying it in, and it did cross my mind that perhaps he was talking to himself, which would have been awkward for both of us. I also remember thinking, for some strange reason, that I should try and look purposeful and put together. As though I had to somehow justify my existence, in my own kitchen, to this stranger who I hadn't invited at all.

I pushed my shoulders back and settled for saying 'Can I help you?' You know, as though he'd just walked straight into a shop and I was there to serve. As though I had soldiers coming into my house at all times of day and night – as though I was used to this kind of thing. But then I realised that he probably didn't speak English, if his whisperings were anything to go by, so I settled for smiling in a way I hoped didn't look like the kind of fake smile you put on for school photographs. My mother had always told me I looked like an idiot in school photographs. She wasn't a lady who would hold back on these things. I was pretty sure she would have told this man to get the hell out of her kitchen if he'd just waltzed in and surprised her in the middle of the night. That, somehow, made me want him to stay.

'Hello,' I said, again, when he didn't reply.

He smiled back, in a way that suggested no words were going to follow, but it didn't seem rude. I wasn't offended by his silence. Quite the opposite. He shuffled his shoes, which were brown and highly polished. He looked very smart.

'Can I get you anything?' I peeled off the rubber gloves I was wearing and walked over to the fridge. 'We've got . . . well . . . it's only casserole,' I shrugged, suddenly wondering why I hadn't cooked a four course meal. 'We've got some left over . . . James wasn't very hungry tonight.' I could hear myself babbling away until I forced myself to stop. It's like that, silence; you want to fill it up because it's a frightening nothing that swallows everything around it. Like a black hole.

The man smiled again and then started walking around the room. He stopped in front of the dresser and picked up a blue vase.

'Oh, that was my mother's,' I said, spooning the casserole into a bowl and shoving it into the microwave. 'She used to collect that kind of old rubbish from car boot sales, but I can't seem to bring myself to throw it away. Stupid, really, don't you think?'

No response.

I tried once more, eyeing his uniform:

'Are you going to go . . . out there, to, well . . . ?' I trailed off. Everyone knew where 'out there' was. That morning's newspaper was on the table, headline pointing to the sky.

He put the vase down, and raised his arms up on either side, straight out, like a cross. I blinked. Then understanding dawned.

'Oh. A plane,' I nodded, and relief flooded through me;

now I knew something. A plane. He flew a plane. Somewhere, for someone, for something. His uniform camouflaged with the sky. 'I love planes,' I heard myself say, stupidly. 'Well. No, actually, that's not true. I'm really not a fan of flying at all. Sorry.'

The microwave *ping*ed. I jumped.

'Here.' I put the bowl and a fork on the kitchen table between us. 'Please do have some. You know, to keep your strength up for flying,' and I found myself spreading out my own arms in imitation before I could stop myself. Like an embarrassing English tourist who speaks loudly on holiday, as though that's going to make the rest of the world understand. Somewhere, my mother rolled her eyes.

Nevertheless, he appeared to laugh, and picked up the bowl and the fork. He eyed them in an interested sort of way and began to eat. He shoved the food into his mouth hurriedly but, again, it wasn't rude. There was even something charming about it, as though he simply hadn't eaten for a long time. I felt pride that he was enjoying my food so much; I'd never really considered myself a good cook before.

He didn't sit down, but continued to stand, glancing up at the light bulbs. This pilot in my kitchen.

'Where are you from?' I chanced, pulling out a chair, and sitting down right on the edge of it.

He looked at me curiously and continued to eat.

'My son is asleep upstairs,' I said to him, changing the subject in case it made him feel uncomfortable. 'Do you have children?'

I pressed on, unable to stay quiet. 'Are you from France?' I tried to remember my GCSE French. I admit I was relieved when he looked puzzled because I couldn't remember much. 'Germany? Holland? Russia?' I started naming countries in Europe, then Asia, South America . . . I remembered James's geography project and wondered if I should fetch his map of the world. Something like pinning the tail on the donkey, but that seemed crude. The pilot scraped the bowl with his fork and winced as though he could hear what I was thinking.

He set the bowl down firmly and nodded. I think it was more of a thank you nod than anything else. He brushed a crumb from his jacket and made towards the door.

'Are you going?' I asked, standing up.

For one wild moment I wondered if perhaps he wasn't a pilot at all but a burglar who was checking out the area in an elaborate ruse, only to come back later and rob me when I'd fallen asleep. It didn't seem likely – but, at that point, what did?

'You can't just walk out and not tell me anything,' I laughed, even though it wasn't the least bit funny. 'I mean, what is this?'

Why my house? I remember thinking, and not saying it.

And why me? I'm just a normal person. Just a normal, everyday person.

He paused at the back door, and I remember thinking, then, that perhaps he did understand what I was saying. Perhaps he knew a lot more than he was letting on and didn't want to say it. Just dropped by to see what it was like, this other existence, this thing he wasn't really part of. Like a changeling, before slipping away into the night. I shivered. In that moment, he reminded me of a man I'd seen walking along the high street with a sign around his neck that says 'The End is Nigh'. This man stamps and cries loudly about the end of the world and all the people hurry by, pretending they can't see him. Pretending they can't hear.

There was something in the pilot's eyes, right then, though I knew I wouldn't be able to explain it properly, to anyone who happened to ask. And, because of that, I knew that I probably wouldn't tell anyone he'd visited. Knew I wouldn't say anything at all. I have a feeling that, in that moment, the pilot knew that, too. And because of that, there was something linking us there, for that small second before he stepped outside of my house and disappeared. Something sad hovering on the air between us, unsaid in the dark.

Margaret and Mary and the
End of the World

Once upon a time, there were four horsemen of the apocalypse.

God breathed them into the world with his fisted right hand.

'I have a bow,' said the white horse. 'I represent Evil.'

'I am War,' said the red horse. 'Mark my sword.'

'I am Famine,' said the black horse. 'And all that comes with it.'

'I am Death,' said the pale horse, who was carrying Hades. 'And this is the end of the whole wide world.'

Sometimes, there is also a beginning.

Mostly. Almost always.

A beginning is wired.

You can trace it with your finger – snake it around your wrist, follow it to the socket, pull it off the wall and peer into the darkness beyond. If you track it further into the murky depths, it will eventually go back to the bottom of the sea. To animals and plants that are stuck between rocks. Between everything and anything and nothing at all.

Your beginning is somewhere in there, crushed together along with everyone else's. The imprint of a dead animal.

You will never find it.

But, sometimes, the beginning is also near your fourteenth birthday. That's where most of my wires go – right into the birthday cake with my mother holding the detonator.

'What are you going to wish for?'

Boom.

That was then.

This is now.

Now I am twenty-eight. I am doubled. My wires spread far and wide, interlinked like the underground and buried just as deep.

I catch the bus, then walk down towards the river. Blackbirds clutter on the corner there. My mother used to sing a song about putting them in a pie. Twenty-four of them with charring feathers. My stomach grumbles. I look at my watch. The gallery closes at ten to six, and they shut her room first because she is one of the oldest.

A girl trapped in a painting, stuck to the wall.

I visit every Friday. The red room she is kept in has air vents lining the floor, and there are twenty-nine people in there with her. Nearby, Ophelia is floating down a river, dead. At the edge of a door, a poet who didn't make it past the age of seventeen. Her world is a collection of scenes that puzzle me. The public walk through it like it's some form of freak show. The people they watch sit behind glass, with name tags by their side and golden frames. They cannot talk, they can only stare.

The painted girl I come to visit is called Mary. She sits in a portrait by Dante Rossetti called *Ecce Ancilla Domini*. It shows her being told she is to give birth to the son of God.

Each time I come to stand in front of this painting, I disappear.

I think of Girl Guides and Church Sundays, carrying flags up to the altar and playing games in the pews. The year we turned eleven, Flora Talbert taught us poker, laying the cards down flat on Mrs Timmins's hand-crocheted prayer mats. We asked God to forgive us for our trespasses as we bluffed our way to victory. Then again, as we forgave those who trespassed against us.

Flora always won.

My mother used to make me go; she said her parents never took her to church when she was young, and sometimes she worried about her own soul. And anyway, she said: it was nice. Sometimes I thought she did it for the recipes she could get from the well-dressed mothers at Sunday school, and because she blushed whenever Reverend David walked by. My mother said he used to give her an extra sip of wine at Holy Communion.

'Such a charming young man,' she said, and hiccoughed.

I remember her sitting in her lilac Sunday best, me in a pair of jeans she'd fashioned into a skirt, when Reverend David told us the story of Mary and Gabriel. I was twelve at the time, and we'd started Greek mythology at school. Liam McGee found a painting in a book of a swan having sex with a lady. The caption said that Greek gods would come down to earth as animals and have sex with women.

'The Greeks were perverts, Margaret,' my mother said. 'Remember that.'

So there we were: gods and women.

Reverend David cleared his throat and beamed. He said that Gabriel had visited Mary and she had been afraid but honoured. He called it a *very blessed event*. He said the word blessed like it was two syllables. *Bless-ed*. Like he was hopping over the word, burning his tongue. We all nodded and clung to our prayer sheets.

Amen.

That winter, my father was made redundant by the Forestry Sector. He sat in the kitchen skewering ham onto cocktail sticks and drank too much beer. Occasionally he'd swear at the telly.

He said it was stress.

'You liquidise what little cash we have!' I heard my mother hiss. 'You're pissing our money down the drain.'

I'd never heard my mother use the word *piss* before.

'Oh, that's rich.'

'Is it?' She slammed a mug down hard. 'Well, I'm glad something is.'

'Oh, you think I'm hiding from all this at the bottom of a pint glass?'

'Too right you are.'

'And what about your chalice, eh?'

'What are you talking about?'

'Supping from the hand of God, eh, Angela?' he laughed nastily. 'Don't think I don't know.'

'You don't know what you're talking about.'

'Well, maybe I'll come along to one of these Bible classes of yours, too, eh? Wednesday nights, isn't it?'

'Yes.' And here I could picture my mother straightening her apron. 'But that's the evening you play darts, dear.'

We had very little money but my mother refused to let anyone know. She said it would make us all the poorer if they did. We had beans and potatoes for three weeks straight and my stomach bloated. My mother spent weekends foraging in the woods that had rejected my father, picking edible berries and piles of nuts.

'I need you to do me a favour, Margaret,' my mother said. 'I need you to stop growing.'

But I was about to turn fourteen. I was growing in all

kinds of places. My mother pretended not to notice. I needed a bra. She said we couldn't afford it.

'It must be jelly, 'cause jam don't shake like that,' Flora giggled, nudging me in the ribs.

'Maybe if you lost some weight you wouldn't grow so fast,' my mother said as she spooned our tiny dinners onto hand-painted plates. 'Now, don't forget to eat your greens.'

'But you said—'

'Now, Margaret, think of all those poor, starving children in Africa,' she said, and she glared at the straining buttons on my blouse, as though I were hoarding all the fat in the world.

I first saw the painting *Ecce Ancilla Domini* tucked inside a poetry book by Christina Rossetti. The painting was printed on a postcard, and on the back someone had written '*Why are Gabriel's feet on fire?*' At the bottom of the postcard it was typed that Christina Rossetti had posed as Mary for her brother to paint her.

The postcard looked as though it had been used as a bookmark, but this was a library book with stamps in the front. The last date said it should have been returned fourteen years before. I wondered what the Reverend would think about my mother stealing poetry books from the local library.

The page it marked said:

Her hair is like the golden corn
A low wind breathes upon
Or like the golden harvest moon
When all the mists are gone.

How skinny and small she looked, I thought.
  How captivating.

In the painting, Mary sits behind two plates of glass, in a white room.

Gabriel stands next to her, at the foot of the bed. His feet are on fire and he is holding out a white lily. A dove floats by his shoulder.

Mary herself is leaning away, against the wall, her legs bunched up under her, looking scared. Behind her is a blue curtain like that around a hospital bed. She is dressed in white.

Gabriel is also dressed in the baggy white of a hospital gown. When I look at them, there is a pain so obvious I can smell it; that very same sensation when you jump into a swimming pool and the water shoots up your nose and tries to reach your brain. The front and back of Gabriel's robes aren't joined at the sides, like a sandwich board, so you can see the naked flesh of his torso.

Beside the bed is a red object, with painted lilies. It looks like a set of scales.

I can see all the bones in Mary's hands. Her sunken

cheeks. Her lollipop head. I imagine Mary as a woman with an eating disorder told she is pregnant in a recovery clinic. She has never undressed in front of a man. She has never slept with a man. The people in this clinic have been starving themselves for God, like nuns in the Middle Ages who would not eat and called it prodigious fasting, saying that they were doing it because they believed it meant they would be able to communicate with God.

Apparitions and fantasies and paper-thin skin.

I remember when I was fourteen and I'd tried so hard to disappear. I had many pockets in my trousers for shoving pieces of food into. I'd stretch up in front of the mirror in the evenings, reach for the ceiling and watch the holes appear in the middle of my ribs. I was a box with a bird inside that got quieter and quieter. I'd crack my knuckles and my knees and give my packed lunch to the homeless man who always sat outside of Tesco.

It was like walking on stilts.

In the summer, with the heat, sometimes I could hear voices. The medieval starving nuns said they were hungry for God. Hungry, starving. They had to stop because the Queen called it heretic. She burned them at the stake, flames licking at their skin. *Bless-ed.* I wonder if people starved themselves in the name of religion before the Middle Ages. I wonder if this is it.

Mary's eyes are staring out of the painting onto the floor.

Why are Gabriel's feet on fire?

The bed is hard, in fact it is a rock. Mary saw them cover it with a sheet before she came in. The women in here are not the same as she is. They are starving so that God will visit them in their sleep. Hannah sleeps next door. She told Mary this morning, over a breakfast they didn't eat, that last night Satan had sat on top of her wardrobe. She said he told her to eat a biscuit.

'And guess what,' she whispered. 'I didn't eat a biscuit.'

On the wall in her room, Mary has cut a series of boxes into the rubble with a stone. There is a cross in each box marking every day before Joseph returns. He made her a boat out of wood, which sits on her bedside table. She is here because he says she has issues. She doesn't eat. He asks her if it is because of God. She has said no – because it's not – she does not know why.

She sits and examines the contours of her wrists. The sun is at its hottest, beating in through the window behind her, and all the nurses are taking their mid-afternoon nap.

Outside, the birds are talking to her.

There is a flash of light.

She jumps.

She is no longer alone.

'Mary,' the angel smiles. 'My name is Gabriel. I am a guardian angel, I bring you news of great joy.'

Mary can't help but notice that the angel's feet are on fire. No wonder it's hot in here. 'Pardon?'

'You shall have a child, Mary! A boy. You are to give him the name Jesus. He will be the son of God.'

'. . . I don't understand.'

The angel smiles, a dove perched on his shoulder. 'You are to have a child; God has chosen you.'

Mary decides that her brain doesn't seem to be working properly. 'This all seems very impossible,' she says. 'I mean, I'm flattered, but I didn't ask to get pregnant.'

'God knows this.'

'And what's my boyfriend going to say?'

'This is the work of God, Mary,' the angel smiles. 'And you must nourish this baby that belongs to him. You must eat, and get well.'

'But I don't—' She begins to think of Hannah, next door, who has talked non-stop about wanting a baby. How none of them can have a baby. All Mary can think of is her stomach swelling. She feels sick. 'But, this is . . . How will I look after the son of God?'

'As you would your own child.'

Mary thinks this should be simple but it isn't. She wonders how many people will believe her: that this angel came into her room and said she was pregnant with the son of God. A baby: a baby growing inside her that belongs to God.

For one ridiculous moment she imagines a baby with a beard.

'This is a very important task, Mary. Very important. You should be thrilled that God has chosen you.'

Mary nods but she feels suddenly empty.

'This is a *bless-ed* event,' Gabriel smiles.

The dove lands on Mary's shoulder, and suddenly she feels as though she is Noah's ark.

It turned out that my mother was right; you could decide not to grow.

When I first stopped eating, she thought it was pious; that I'd started listening to her talk of aid and starving children in Africa; she said that everything I didn't eat she'd bundle up and send to someone who needed it more.

'Spread the fat around,' she said, patting my back. 'That's my girl.'

I pinned my hair up in front of the mirror and sucked in my cheeks. Balloon head. My choices were eating me. I was sure if you shone a light on my head you'd be able to see the bones in my skull.

Sometimes, if I skipped several meals, my head swam so much I could hear the birds talking. A dove sat on the windowsill. I smiled at the dinner table and tried to pretend my stomach wasn't trying to gnaw its way through my skin to get to the food on my plate.

'Amazing,' my mother said, and packaged the food away.

Flora introduced me to whisky on a Wednesday night when we were supposed to be at Girl Guides. Her parents were away for the week. We drank a whole bottle. We were so wasted that we ripped up her bed sheets and wound them around ourselves like dead Egyptians.

'You're so skinny, Margaret.' She picked up one of my arms but I couldn't feel her fingers. I enjoyed these out-of-body experiences. I enjoyed trying on other people. We danced to terrible music, wrapped up in white.

Eventually, we collapsed on the living-room carpet, staring up at the ceiling.

'Have you ever, you know?' she asked.

There were rumours she'd done it with Liam McGee.

'No,' I said, like I didn't have the time.

She picked my arm up again. 'Probably for the best; you'd snap in two.'

We giggled into our glasses. Me: the shrinking tree.

I got home just after midnight. My mother was up and waiting, sitting on the doorstep, smoking a cigarette and trying to look calm.

'What the hell do you think you look like?'

I looked down at myself and shrugged, trying not to laugh.

'Behold,' I said. 'I am the Holy Spirit. On spirits.'

I spun in circles, allowing the white sheets to billow out around me. My mother simply sat, watching me, blowing smoke into the night air.

I stopped and vomited violently into the gutter.

'Right.' She stubbed out her cigarette on the white-washed walls. 'That's quite enough of that.'

I was dragged to the Reverend's house first thing next morning, dazed and hungover, where she told him she was scared I was turning into a demon. She said I wouldn't eat, that she'd thought it was for the common good, but that now she wasn't so sure. She used phrases she'd heard on TV that she'd never said out loud in her life, like 'going over the edge' and 'problem child' and 'completely self-absorbed'.

Her mouth seemed to move at a different speed to the rest of her body.

I was only half listening. I was imagining the white cliffs of Dover. The white doves. Falling over the side.

'I think you'd best come in, Margaret,' the Reverend winked at me. 'Don't worry, Angela. I'll sort all this out.'

He shut the door in my mother's face.

'So, what appears to be the problem, Margaret?'

'I can hear the birds,' I said. His hand was on the small of my back as he guided me into his living room. 'Do you think that if you shone a light on my face you'd be able to see my skull?'

'You mean like a halo?' he laughed, and poured me a drink.

There is a man in the gallery who has sidled up beside me. I don't like how close he is.

'Beautiful painting, isn't it?' he says.

I try not answering, to see if he will leave.

'Sad, though, don't you think?'

I can't help it: 'What's sad?'

'Well,' he smiles at me, the tips of his fingers resting on his chin. 'The piece itself, really: the history.' He keeps glancing at me while he talks. 'You know that the artist asked his sister to pose as Mary for him, she—'

'Christina Rossetti, yes.' I want him to realise that I know this painting.

'Yes,' he nods. 'She was a problem child.'

We look at the painting, at Mary shying away from someone she should trust. I look down and notice that the man is wearing orange trainers.

'Mary's halo and Gabriel's halo are different colours,' I say. 'Because Gabriel's halo was added three years after the painting was first exhibited. Critics thought he didn't look angelic enough.'

The man looks impressed.

'I often look for God in this picture,' he said. 'Do you believe in God?'

'That's not the point, is it?'

'Isn't it?'

'No, it's not.' I wish he'd disappear. I close my eyes and count to ten.

Christina Rossetti was born in London in 1830. Her father was an exiled Italian revolutionary and her brothers were famous artists. She had a collection of poems published by her grandfather at the age of twelve and, two years after that, was said to have had a nervous breakdown due to religious mania. In her late teens, she posed for her brother, Dante, several times, dressed as Mary. As an adult, she spent ten years volunteering at a Mary Magdalene Asylum for Fallen Women. She died in 1894.

Each time I come to the gallery I manage to see a different painting. Sometimes it's me, sometimes it's Mary, sometimes it's Christina. Once Gabriel was a dustbin man coming for a weekly collection. Like an out-of-sync period. 'I have come for blood. I will give you blood: family. I will give you the blood of Christ. Body and Soul.'

I continue to stare straight on until all of the colours blur. I imagine Christina reciting her poetry:

> We must not look at goblin men,
> We must not buy their fruits:

Who knows upon what soil they fed
Their hungry thirsty roots?

'So, I see the Reverend every Tuesday now,' I told Flora.

'What's he going to do?' she asked.

'He says he's going to unpeel me like a fruit to get to the core of all my problems,' I said. 'Don't you think that's funny?'

'I guess.'

'I mean, it's like he's reaching into my soul . . . or something.'

'Right.' She continued to braid my hair in silence.

Flora and I had a mutual understanding.

We didn't speak of the unspeakable things.

It turned out I didn't quite snap in two.

I bent.

I changed.

I didn't have a Gabriel.

I was told by a pregnancy test. By that little line turning pink.

I handed it wordlessly to Flora.

'Blimey,' she said.

And we stared at the floor.

I had a dream that my stomach was the world. That Reverend David lifted it up, clean off my body, and held it aloft for the congregation to see. They all started to sing 'He's got the whole world . . . in his hands . . . he's got the whole wide world . . .' and then I looked down at myself and realised that I was bleeding to death.

After five months, when I couldn't hide it any longer, I told my mother.

I said it was Liam McGee but I don't know if she believed me. She asked if his family had Greek ancestry. Then she lit a cigarette and tapped her foot. She even poured herself a beer.

'You know what, Angela?' my dad said, frowning at my stomach. 'You should have bought that girl a bloody bra!'

I was told I was to give the baby up. My mother said it was the right thing to do. I was too scared to disagree with her. The doctor told me I had to stay in bed for weeks. I wasn't well. He said that I shouldn't have been able to get pregnant in the first place, really; he said I was too thin. He said I was malnourished. He said I had to eat. My mother liked the fact I had to stay in bed; it meant the neighbours didn't get a chance to see much of me.

When I looked at myself in the mirror, I felt like a cage. I felt like the stork.

'You're going to do this wonderful, selfless thing,' my mother said, sewing an elastic band into my trousers.

'You're going to give a baby to a couple who've always wanted a child but could never have one. Don't you think that's a wonderful thing to do, Margaret?'

'Very saintly,' I remember saying and I thought she was going to slap me.

'You know we can't afford another mouth to feed, Margaret.'

Outside we could hear horses, their hooves clattering on the tarmac.

'Did I ever tell you about the four horsemen of the apocalypse?' she said, and started sewing again, as though the piece of material was a person she was stabbing repeatedly in the heart.

The baby kicked.

'Yes,' I said. 'Thousands of times.'

'Oh,' she said, recovering quickly. 'In that case, let me tell you this one . . .'

> What does the bee do?
> Bring home honey.
> And what does Father do?
> Bring home money.
> And what does Mother do?
> Lay out the money.
> And what does baby do?
> Eat up the honey.

One night I had a dream that my mother made a scarecrow. I went downstairs to get a glass of milk and she was shoving straw inside one of the suits she'd collected for Christian Aid. She said that she was trying to make the demons go away. She stuffed it so full that it split at the seams, and then gave it a carrot for a nose. She snapped it so that the end broke. It dangled pathetically.

'Right, let's get this outside,' and she dragged it right into the middle of her vegetable patch, next to the aubergines that had won her first prize at the church fair, even though Mrs Timmins's were better.

She pulled a box of matches from her pocket and lit one. She set fire to the legs of the scarecrow, letting the smoke billow out around her. She looked like a figure from a murder mystery film as I stood watching her from the doorway.

'That's right!' she shrieked at the scarecrow. 'You stay where you are until you're all gone!' And suddenly she wasn't my mother anymore. She was Mary Tudor. 'Heresy!' she cried, as the flames burned white.

The scarecrow screamed. My non-mother danced.

I woke up, sweating, with cramp in my legs.

By January, my stomach was so huge I used to pretend it was a map. The veins under my skin were rivers. I'd trace them in bed and read them poems. These were my baby's wires, winding their way around the equator, deep beneath the sea.

Flora came to visit me sometimes, when my mother was out, and my dad let her in. We played snap.

'Did you hear?' she said, dealing out the cards.

'Hear what?'

'We got a new vicar.'

'Oh,' I said, carefully. 'What's he like?'

'Dunno,' she shrugged. 'Old, I suppose. But the other guy left in a hurry.'

'Yeah?'

'Yeah. He had to move out 'cause his house was burned down.'

MARGARET (name)

meaning: 'a pearl', 'the bud of a flower' or 'daughter of light'.

Other variants of Margaret are: Maggie, Madge, Marge, Meg, Megan, Rita, Daisy, Greta, Gretel, Gretchen, Magee, Mary, Molly, Meggie, Peggy and Peg.

Once upon a time there was a boy called Hansel and a girl called Gretel. They were the children of a woodcutter. But their father had lost his job and they were very, very poor.

Their mother was a rather wicked lady.

'We cannot keep these children,' she said to their father.

'It is too expensive. We must take them into the middle of the forest and leave them there. I'm sure they'll be able to survive on their own. Children are very inventive.'

And because the father was bewitched by this woman, he said: 'Yes, let's. We'll make a day of it.'

And so they did. They told Hansel and Gretel that they were going to take them on a picnic in the centre of the forest. The children were very excited; they'd never been on a picnic before.

But that night Hansel and Gretel overheard their parents talking about their plan to abandon them.

'Hush,' said the sister. 'We will take some bread and drop crumbs out behind us so we can follow them all the way home.'

So they pulled pieces of the stale bread between their fingers and let them hit the ground behind them as they walked.

'Here we are!' Their mother spread her arms out wide in the middle of the woods. 'How wonderful. Oh wait, what's that, over there?'

Hansel and Gretel turned to look and, when they turned back, their parents had gone. It was so quick that Gretel wondered if they'd turned into trees.

'Where's the bread?'

But they saw a large blackbird eating the last of the bread they had dropped. So they were stuck.

After wandering through the woods for hours, they saw

smoke in the distance. It was coming out of a chimney. The house the chimney was on top of was a strange house. It was made out of gingerbread and honey and cherries and nuts. Hansel's stomach rumbled.

'Let's go and look!'

As they approached the front door, it opened and a lady came out. She was old and looked oddly familiar. She was very happy to see the children.

'Come on in, my dears,' she coaxed, and in they went.

But as soon as they were in the house, the woman slammed the door behind them.

Boom!

She grabbed Hansel and turned him into a bird, then threw him in a cage. He squawked in anger. Then the woman turned to Gretel and said she was going to feed her up. She said that she looked too thin. Gretel tried to run, but found her hands and legs were locked in chains. The woman made her sit on the floor, and she force-fed her:

pomegranates full and fine
dates and sharp bullaces
rare pears and greengages
damsons and bilberries
currants and gooseberries
bright-fire-like barberries

and Gretel watched her stomach get bigger and bigger and bigger until she thought she was going to burst.

She cradled her stomach like it was the world.

'Now,' said the woman, when she had fed Gretel non-stop for four days and four nights. 'Now you are ready to go in the oven.'

The oven was the mouth of the kitchen. The woman began to sing. 'Sing a song of sixpence, a pocket full of rye. Let's stuff this little girl into a pie . . .'

Gretel, her eyes so small in her swollen face, noticed a broom sidling up beside her.

'Use me!' it whispered.

So she did. Gretel managed to grab it between her chained-up hands and she waited until the woman had opened the oven and then pushed with all her might, shoving her in the back with the broom. The woman fell into the oven with a bang and a scream.

The smell of burning flesh was overpowering.

The spell was broken.

The cage and chains disappeared. Hansel turned back into a boy, Gretel grabbed his hand and they ran out of the house that was made of gingerbread and honey and cherries and nuts. They ran into the forest, and then all the way home, hope leading the way.

Their father was sitting outside their house in a deck-chair, playing solitaire. He was very pleased to see them.

He said that their mother had died unexpectedly in the night, and he was extremely sorry that he had tried to abandon them both in the woods.

They all sang and danced and had a big roast supper. Their father sharpened his carving knife for the occasion. They all tucked in.

'Daddy, what kind of meat is this?' Gretel asked, a big chunk of it stuck in her teeth.

'A new kind,' her father said, calmly cutting it up into very small pieces. 'Now, don't forget to eat your greens.'

The man next to me in the gallery has moved on. I can see him looking back at me every so often as though he thinks I'm crazy.

The assistants are beginning to move around the gallery, tapping people on the shoulder, saying that they're about to close up. That it's time to go.

Mary is standing by the sink, folding the ironing. She has thirty minutes until her taxi arrives. The taxi that will take her to the clinic. She's sewn coins into the waistband of her jeans, one-pound coins that line her hips with gold, like a halo. A chastity belt. She'll also drink two litres of water at the end of the taxi ride, if she can hold it in. That will help. She folds clothes, the bones of her wrists flashing upwards.

'Hey. How's it going?'

Mary nearly jumps out of her transparent skin. There is a man sitting at the kitchen table.

She can't help but notice that his feet are on fire.

'Who the hell are you? How did you get in here?'

'Always be prepared, that's my motto,' and he holds his hands up in fake surrender.

'I didn't hear you break in!'

'Mary, Mary.' He flashes her a winning smile. 'I made myself a spare key. Cuts down on all the divine apparition. You know, sometimes it's nice to do things the human way. I'm an angel, you see.'

Mary doesn't know what to say. She doesn't know whether to call the police. Or perhaps the fire brigade.

Or perhaps she's just seeing things again.

'I've got an appointment soon, you know,' she says. 'So perhaps you should leave.'

But Gabriel doesn't leave. Mary tries to pretend he isn't there. She turns back to the ironing and starts singing to herself. 'Sing a song of sixpence, a pocket full of rye, four and twenty blackbirds . . .'

But then Gabriel begins to sing too: 'Mary, Mary, quite contrary. How does your garden grow?'

She glares at him but he doesn't stop.

'With silver bells and cockle shells and pretty maids all in a row . . . Do you realise that that's a song about mass execution?'

'It's about a garden . . .'

'No. It's about Mary Tudor, and her massacre of the Protestants. Her garden is her graveyard.' The angel seems to take great pleasure in telling her this, and rummages through her fruit bowl as he continues. 'Yes, silver bells are thumbscrews and cockleshells were torture devices used for, well, you know.' He gestures to his crotch. 'And as for "pretty maids all in a row", maid was the name for the guillotine.'

'Oh.' Mary's face falls.

Gabriel looks pleased with himself. 'And ring-a-ring-o'-roses was a song about the plague. My, my, the things parents get their children to sing about, eh? Anyway, down to business. You're pregnant, congratulations.'

'Pardon?'

'Yep, you know, son of God, inside you. Perhaps the daughter of God if we're, you know, moving with the times,' and he laughs as though he doesn't really think so. 'Great stuff.'

'Do I get a say in this?'

Gabriel laughs louder. 'Sorry, I appear to have set fire to your tablecloth.'

I gave birth to her on a Friday, and she was gone by the Sunday. I wasn't told what they called her; my mother said that it was best I didn't know. She thought that naming things made you form a bond with them.

'Like Adam and the world,' she said.

I didn't know what to say.

I used to wonder what would have happened if Mary had handed her baby to a stranger and told them to raise it. I think of Zeus and his many earthling children. I think of my mother, now, all these years later, acting like a child herself who no longer knows its name.

I step out of the gallery, surprised by how dark it is. The building stands right on the edge of the Thames. Blue lights are twisted along the front of the Tate into letters, which declare: 'Everything is going to be all right.'

A man is taking a photo of it on his phone. It seems smug – this new version of a 'message from above' engineered by scaffolding, powered by electricity, shared on the Internet. Wireless technology, that's our myth now. Telling ourselves stories that wrap around the globe. Viral whispers, buzz, buzz, buzzing.

I wonder where all the wires go.

I try one last time when I get to the nursing home.

'Mum, about those adoption papers . . .' but she's not even listening. She's looking at a pigeon sitting on the windowsill. Then she waves at a nurse walking by. Her nightgown flaps by her side.

'Do you remember what I said?' she says, suddenly, as though she's just realised I'm there.

'What about?' I ask.

'About my cremation,' she says. 'After I'm gone. I want an open-top cremation, out in the countryside – near the woods; they've made a law so you can do that now.' She closes her eyes, breathing heavily. After a minute I wonder if she's fallen asleep, but then her eyes snap back open. 'Yes. I want four horses to draw the funeral cart.' She sounds lucid for the first time in weeks. 'I want to go out in flames with everyone watching . . .' She laughs to herself. 'You can set fire to my feet first, if you like.'

Little Deaths

Our town is full of ghosts.

We try to catch them during break. They struggle against our grip, shapeshifting. We shove them into wine bottles and jam jars, fish bowls and snow globes. Henry tries trapping one in a fruit basket but it slowly leaks out through the cracks, making a pool of ominous red that evaporates with a giggle. Henry always catches the most but he's taller than the rest of us, so I call it cheating.

We give these ghosts to the teachers, who give them to the government, but I always manage to smuggle a few of them home. I have a hidden compartment at the base of my wheelchair that no one ever checks.

My mother and I sell some of these captured spirits at the market.

Ghosts in jars light up the streets on Saturday mornings, swinging from tarpaulin, ready to be sold as medicine and prayers. The priest-doctors weave between the stalls with tape measures, light meters and necklaces hung with IOUs. I write messages on the glass with the tips of my fingers and watch the mist disappear, never knowing if the air has swallowed it or the ghost inside has gobbled it up.

'Can you hear me?' I scrawl.

I look for the ghost's eyes. I want to know if it can see me; if it's peering out at the world through crackled fog. I wonder what it's thinking. They come in all different colours, these ghosts. The purple ones go for the highest price: slippery poltergeists. Some sellers use food dye to make exotic rainbow spirits – the brighter the better – but often the colours split or the ghost is allergic, growing and growing until it breaks through the glass and out into the air with a sigh of relief. An aggressive little ghost balloon.

The fakers always get caught in the end.

At the market, the nearest priest-doctor starts haggling with Henry's dad over a violet spirit in a marmalade jar.

'I'll give you three and a blessing,' he says, and then catches me staring, so I scramble out of my wheelchair and pull myself under the counter. I can still spy him beneath the tablecloth but he can't see me.

Government priest-doctors, like this one, believe that the ghosts are pockets of death which can be manipulated in labs, edited and liquidised. They claim that one of these days they'll be able to use them to inject us with immortality. And then these ghosts that we accidentally birth inside ourselves, and hiccough out several times a day, will disappear for good.

Then we will be empty.

Right now, we are ghost hotels.

I prop myself up on dusty pillows and pull my homework out of my bag.

English:

How would you like to die? Please number your preferences 1–10, with 1 being the most preferable. You have a 1000 word limit. You will be marked on your ability to persuade.

Maths:

How much should your family and friends cry at your funeral? You have a limit of 1000 tears. Please share these out among those you expect to attend. Show your working.

Biology:

Draw a pair of infected lungs and label them correctly.

Philosophy:

What is death? What does it mean to be alive? Discuss.

I pick up a purple pencil and draw a pair of lungs that look like squashed sausages with tiny ghosts brewing at the base. I cough and clamp my hands over my mouth but an orange wisp escapes and I taste lemons.

Just a half ghost. Just a whisper.

Above me, my mother is starting to argue with someone I know she'll refuse to serve.

Illegal scientists, like my mother, love the ghosts. She goes on expeditions across poppy fields and cliffs, secretly taking photographs, which she develops in special chemicals. We stick them on the basement walls, all sizes and colours and fantastic shapes. Sometimes my mother invites these spirits home for dinner and I get to feed them their favourite food: electricity. They hum and fizz like jellyfish and dance around in circles. Then they giggle, giggle, giggle. We record their sounds and guess their names before they fly away.

The only ghosts we sell at the market are the ones I steal from school. Mum says we have to have a stall for show, but we only sell to jar-breakers. Not to priest-doctors or witches or anyone else. Though once I gave a ghost to a very old man who said he needed company. I told him to open the jar when he got home, introduce himself calmly and see if the ghost wanted to stay.

I think about him sometimes. I wonder how he's getting on.

History:
Do you feel the presence of the past in your breath?

My grandma used to sit me on her knee to tell me stories about the early ghosts. The first one she'd ever seen hovered over the Green Sea, like fog. Except it moved with purpose and it was magenta, and when she closed her eyes she could hear it singing in a language she'd never heard before.

'I think that ghost came from another country,' Grandma said. 'Some shipwrecked spirit, roaming. Looking for another home.'

Then came reports of ghosts interfering with radio waves, floating through TV screens. An Other, from goodness knows where, until we realised we'd started birthing them ourselves. Like cold breath in the morning, except, with that breath, a memory escaped, too. A little part of us, pushed into the air: up, up and away.

'And here we are,' my grandma whispered, surrounded by ghosts. One hugged her chest, and she patted its head. 'Some say we've become ugly. They think that we're dying. I say: look at all the colours, floating in the air.'

The Beginning of the World
in the Middle of the Night

It's 3 a.m. Everything's quiet, bar the sound of a clock on the bedroom wall. JULIAN is in bed. EVELYN is sitting by the window, looking out at the garden.

EVELYN [whispers]: Julian . . . Psst. Julian!
[Pause]
EVELYN [louder]: *JULIAN!*
[There's a thump as EVELYN throws a pillow at the bed. JULIAN stirs]
JULIAN: Huh?
EVELYN: Have you looked at the tree?
JULIAN [yawning]: What?
EVELYN: The apple tree, outside. Have you looked at it?
JULIAN: Apple tree   ?
EVELYN: Yes.
JULIAN: Evelyn . . . It's . . . it's *three* in the morning!
EVELYN: Well, *that's* not answering my question.
JULIAN: It's answer enough for three in the morning. I'm not getting out of bed to come and stare at a tree.
EVELYN: Fine.

[Pause]

JULIAN: What's so exciting about it, anyway?

EVELYN: I love this tree, you know I do.

JULIAN: I do?

EVELYN: It's the one you proposed under.

JULIAN: Oh, that one. Is there any particular reason you're staring at it? I can't imagine it's doing much.

EVELYN: That's exactly what it's doing. Absolutely nothing. I'm just trying to catch it off guard.

JULIAN [confused]: Well, once you've worked out how to catch a tree off guard, please do let me know. Come on, come back to bed. You've got to be up early tomorrow. Well, *today*.

EVELYN: I know, but this is just – it's been bugging me. You pruned the branches and they're already sprouting back again.

JULIAN: That's what trees do, Evelyn. You've got to cut them back so they can grow.

EVELYN: But I've never witnessed this tree actually growing. It was simply not there at all, and then suddenly – bam – it's everywhere.

JULIAN: Things creep up on you.

EVELYN: Hmmm.

JULIAN: Come to bed.

EVELYN: But . . . Where do you think it begins?

JULIAN: Where does what begin?

EVELYN: The tree. Keep up.

JULIAN: Oh.

EVELYN: When did it begin growing, I mean? It was in the garden before we moved in, but I don't know if it's been on the earth longer than we have, for instance. How could we find that out? Is there a record somewhere?

JULIAN: . . . I don't know.

EVELYN: Where does anything begin, anyway? Where do things start?

JULIAN: I'm too tired to think about it.

EVELYN: All beginnings begin at their beginnings, where they belong.

JULIAN: Right.

EVELYN: There are many beginnings, though. Somewhere, underground, there should be a massive row of filing cabinets, winding and branching out across the country. And each of them should contain everyone's – and everything's – beginnings. Labelled properly. Correctly. Where we can see them.

JULIAN [sarcastically]: Underground, where we can see them?

EVELYN: You know, you're very talkative for someone who can't be bothered to get out of bed to look at a tree, worrying about me having to 'get up early tomorrow morning'.

JULIAN: Not tomorrow, *today*.

EVELYN: Whatever. Where do days begin?

JULIAN: Now you're just being silly.

[Pause]

EVELYN: I think, tomorrow—

JULIAN: —today?

EVELYN: Today. I'm going to write our names on our tree outside.

JULIAN: Why?

EVELYN: I'll use one of the kitchen knives.

JULIAN: Don't go using one of my good knives; you'll ruin it. Anyway, I thought you'd be worried about hurting that bloody tree, seeing as you love it so much.

EVELYN: They're made of strong stuff.

[Pause]

EVELYN [sighing]: They won't cut it down, will they?

JULIAN: I don't know. There was another letter through about it today.

EVELYN: Did you read it?

JULIAN: I skimmed it. It's downstairs somewhere.

EVELYN: Where?

JULIAN: I don't know. Somewhere. I'll find it in the morning.

EVELYN: They can't cut it down. It has great sentimental value. And they definitely and absolutely can't cut it down if it has our names written on it. That would be like taking an axe to our souls.

JULIAN: That's a bit dramatic.

EVELYN: It would be, though. Carving our names into the wood would indicate that the tree contains our inner selves. As though we'd put them into another living thing. For safekeeping.

JULIAN: Hardly safekeeping if there's a threat of said tree being cut down by the council.

EVELYN: That man next door is such a pathetic git. What was it he said? That the branches block his sunlight? Well. It's our sunlight, or lack thereof, too, and I enjoy both that *and* our tree in equal measure.

JULIAN: You would. But that's not what he's saying. He's saying that the roots of the tree are going into his garden and are damaging the base of his house.

EVELYN: Evil man. Making up rubbish.

JULIAN: Evelyn, he says that his living-room floor is beginning to tilt.

EVELYN: He probably only thinks that because he spends his afternoons drinking. Everything tilts to him. He can't even walk straight.

JULIAN: Now I think *you're* talking rubbish, Evelyn.

EVELYN: I have seen that man drinking!

JULIAN: When?

EVELYN: Well, I er . . . He drank that wine we offered him when we invited him over for our house-warming a few years ago.

JULIAN: I seem to remember you drinking your fair share of wine that night, too.

EVELYN: Yes, but I'm not the one who says her living-room floor is tilting.

JULIAN: That's because ours isn't.

EVELYN: Hmmm.

[Pause]

EVELYN: Julian?

JULIAN: . . . Yes?

EVELYN: Are you still awake?

JULIAN: . . . No.

EVELYN: Oh.

[Pause]

EVELYN: Julian?

JULIAN: . . .YES?

EVELYN: I think you're lying.

[JULIAN sighs]

JULIAN: OK, fine. I'm absolutely awake. What is it you want to talk about?

[EVELYN climbs back into bed, gleefully]

EVELYN: I want to talk about beginnings.

JULIAN: Fine. Once upon a time . . .

EVELYN: This isn't a bedtime story.

JULIAN: Heavens above, and here was I thinking I was in a bed. What a fool.

[EVELYN giggles]

EVELYN: A complete fool. So, are you sitting comfortably?

JULIAN: No.

EVELYN: Excellent. So. In the beginning . . . there was nothing.

JULIAN: Nothing?

EVELYN: Nothing at all. Nothing apart from the darkness and the stars.

JULIAN: Stars aren't nothing.

EVELYN: OK, OK, there were no stars. I'll put them out with a cosmic fire extinguisher.

JULIAN: You don't have a cosmic fire extinguisher – nothing exists.

EVELYN: You are *ruining* this story.

[JULIAN laughs]

EVELYN: So. In the beginning. Where there was nothing and no stars and no cosmic fire extinguishers to even put out metaphorical stars—

JULIAN: —hang on.

EVELYN: What now?

JULIAN: Surely a beginning is something, too.

EVELYN: Well, I—

JULIAN: A beginning denotes a period in time, and, for you to pinpoint it, time must exist, and if time exists then something exists. So, therefore, thus and henceforth, there is no such thing as nothing.

EVELYN: But—

JULIAN: It's true, you know it's true.

EVELYN: No, no, no – there was no one there to witness time because nothing was there. And if nothing was there to witness it—

JULIAN: You mean, if a tree falls in a forest and no one is around to hear it?

EVELYN: Exactly. And don't talk about trees falling down.

JULIAN: Sorry.

EVELYN: So, am I allowed to continue?

JULIAN [yawning]: I suppose.

EVELYN: Thank you. So . . . In the beginning . . . In the beginning there was nothing. Not a ripple moved throughout the universe because there were no atoms, and there was no energy. And then – because that's always how things go – and then. And then there was something. It was a dream. Dreams don't need atoms to form themselves because they are made of something less definite. They are able to form out of air that is only just on the brink of existing behind the darkness. The very thought of air. Nobody knows who dreamed the dream, or where it came from. Perhaps it was a dream that floated over from another world, no one knows. It was *ex nihilo nihil fit*: out of nothing comes nothing. And that was OK, because this was a time before the word *logic* had been formed. Before the alphabet had been carved out of stone and time, and before we, as humans, had even started to think of existing. The possibility of us, and of all life, was sleeping. And we emerged from a dream.

[Pause]

EVELYN: And because we come from a dream, we never really know if we're awake.

JULIAN [sarcastically]: I know I'm awake right now.

EVELYN: If you can do better, then I'd like to hear it.

JULIAN: You want to hear my story on beginnings?

EVELYN: Yes, I do.

JULIAN: And then I can go to sleep?

EVELYN: I'll consider it.

JULIAN: Right. OK, here goes.

EVELYN: And you're not allowed to be logical in your beginnings.

JULIAN [clearing his throat]: OK . . . OK. In the beginning . . . In the beginning there were several worlds. They were sewn together like the pages of a book you could walk through, and each footstep took you through to another world. It was like stepping onto the first page of a new story. And in one of those stories, there was a man. But the man hadn't always been a man. He had been born out of a star, and that star had been thrown out of a black hole. Spat out, saliva and all, into the navy expanse of nothing. The star pulsed with its own energy, propelled about the universe at high speed because there was nothing to stop it. It was free. And because it was free, it was able to think. And because it could think, it could will things to happen. The star willed itself to slow down and it began to lose speed, gradually, until it stopped, in one spot, at the far end of the universe, looking out over the darkness. The star was amazed by the sheer vastness of what it saw, and it was afraid. And because it was afraid, it meant it had something it feared losing, and that, in turn, meant that it could love.

EVELYN: Love?

JULIAN: Shhh. Over time, the star changed from a star into a heart. The heart pulsed light out across the universe, and from that heart grew limbs, one by one – until it was a man.

EVELYN: Not a woman?

JULIAN: This is my story.

EVELYN: Sorry.

JULIAN: The heart grew until it was a man. This man was the first man to see the universe. He looked around, and didn't think he liked it much. There was nothing there. So, he started imagining a world that had things in it. A world that had trees—

EVELYN [interrupting]: How did he know what trees were, if he'd never seen one before?

JULIAN: I thought I wasn't allowed to use logic.

EVELYN: I know, but—

JULIAN: This is reverse creation, Evelyn. Things existed in this world because he thought of them.

EVELYN: Oh, how clever, that a man thought up everything in the world. And were there people native to this world that he'd conveniently forgotten about? That he had perhaps killed off with a thought?

JULIAN: Evelyn.

EVELYN: Hmmm.

JULIAN [trying to continue with the story]: There was a man . . . !

EVELYN: OK, OK.

JULIAN: There was a man who thought of trees. And he thought that he'd like to walk among them, so he moved one step forward and suddenly he was surrounded by trees. But it was dark. So, he thought that the world needed something to give him light. He stepped forward again and the world changed into a place that was lit by a thousand stars in the sky. They glowed orange over all of the trees – it was beautiful. But there was nothing to eat, and nothing to drink, and, because the man was thinking about these things, he suddenly realised that he was thirsty, and hungry. So he stepped forward again and there were vegetables, and also water, and fish in the sea. Yes, the sea. The sea was another thing that he had imagined – a shade lighter than the navy sky that hung above it.

EVELYN: And then, in this new world, he found a woman.

JULIAN: Are you taking over my story?

EVELYN: Yes. It's time for my beginning. There was once

a world that a woman owned. She had formed it through years *and years* of hard work and imagination. It was amazing. It was out of this world. She looked around her, at the trees, and the land, and the sea. She sat down, cross-legged, and started to make a fire with a stick and a stone. At that very moment, a man stepped out from between the trees. He was gazing at the sea as though he'd never seen anything like it in his life.

'Hi,' the woman said, getting to her feet. 'I've been waiting for you. I've been here a long time, actually – where the hell have you been?'

[Pause]

JULIAN: I supposed I asked for that.

EVELYN: Yes, I suppose you did.

JULIAN: OK. How about this one? In the beginning there were several beginnings, and they were all talking at once, because they all wanted to be heard. They talked louder and louder, their words crossing and colliding with each other so forcefully that it built up a large amount of pressure. This pressure expanded out across all the beginnings and pressed down on their ears, growing and gaining more power from all the conflicting stories until, quite suddenly, it exploded into a massive ball of fire. A fire that coiled itself into a snake. Everything was orange. And from all that energy, the world was born.

[Pause]

EVELYN: You can't say that.

JULIAN: I can't say what?

EVELYN: That the world was born out of conflict and hatred.

JULIAN: Plenty of good things come about because of bad things, Evelyn. That doesn't, in turn, make them bad.

EVELYN: Well, it's not very nice.

[Pause]

EVELYN: Julian?

JULIAN: Mmm?

EVELYN: What if this is our beginning?

JULIAN: What do you mean?

EVELYN: I mean, what if this is our beginning, right here, now, in this bed, in this room, in this house?

JULIAN: It can't be; we're not babies.

EVELYN: There are many different types of beginnings. And who's to say we haven't imagined our lives up to this point? Who's to say we haven't been propelled into this world from a parallel universe? One that's just come into existence? This could be the very beginning of it, now. I mean, there's no one else here. Listen. It's completely quiet.

JULIAN: But—

EVELYN: No, listen.

[They both fall silent. The clock ticks in the background]

EVELYN: Can you hear that?

JULIAN: Hear what? The clock?

EVELYN: No, that's just time. Time's always there. What else can you hear? Listen.

JULIAN: I can't hear anything.

EVELYN: Exactly. Nothing. We are the only people here. In this room. What's outside of this room?

JULIAN: . . . Our house.

EVELYN: Is it? Have you checked recently?

JULIAN: I don't need to look outside the bedroom door to check to see if our house is still there.

EVELYN: Then I'm not sure you understand how the world works.

JULIAN: I understand how *my* world works. I'm not sure what planet you're on.

EVELYN: Our planet. Our very own. What is it John Donne said: 'For love, all love of other sights controls. And makes one little room an everywhere.'

[JULIAN scoffs]

JULIAN: You should get that printed on a Valentine's Day card.

EVELYN: At this rate, I won't be sending that card to you.

JULIAN: Cards, Evelyn. Paper. That requires people to cut down trees.

EVELYN: An e-card then.

JULIAN: What is this, 1997? And, anyway, there's no computer in this room – which is apparently our world.

So I think you might be screwed. No card, no e-card, no sending of love poems to me or to anyone else.

EVELYN: Then I shall recite one to you. A one-woman show.

JULIAN: Can't wait.

EVELYN: A show for us. The two of us. The only people in the whole wide world.

JULIAN: Like a new Adam and Eve?

EVELYN: Quite. [She clears her throat] In the beginning, it was silent . . .

[The phone on the bedside table starts ringing. They both look at it in disbelief]

JULIAN: Who the hell is that?

EVELYN: I know. We're supposed to be the only ones who exist!

JULIAN: That's not what I meant. I meant it's three thirty in the morning.

[They stare at the ringing phone]

EVELYN: Maybe . . . maybe it's God.

JULIAN: Oh, yes, all angry at us for making up different beginnings to the world. [Pause] I'm going to answer it.

EVELYN: Don't. I should be asleep.

JULIAN: Yes, but for some miraculous reason, you're not. [JULIAN reaches out to pick up the receiver. EVELYN stops him]

EVELYN: Please don't. It's probably just my sister.

JULIAN: Your sister?

EVELYN: Yes. She's developed an annoying habit of calling me at all hours of the day and night to see if I'm OK.

JULIAN: That's ridiculous. Why wouldn't you be?

EVELYN: Exactly. I'm fine.

[They both stare at the phone. It stops ringing]

EVELYN: Hopefully she'll think I didn't answer because I'm asleep, like a normal person.

JULIAN: You're not a normal person.

EVELYN: I'll take that as a compliment.

[There is a long pause]

JULIAN: Speaking of phone calls, I saw there was a voice mail, earlier, left by our dear next-door neighbour.

EVELYN: What did he want?

JULIAN: He wanted to check that you'd received the letter about 'that blasted tree' destroying his house.

EVELYN: Yes, well, I'll bloody burn his letter.

JULIAN: He seems to think that you're not taking this seriously. That grief is driving you mad.

EVELYN: Not taking this seriously? He's trying to murder our tree; I'm taking that very seriously. He's a moron! And I hate him. He can stick it, and his letter, and his complaint to the local council. I bet there's nothing wrong with his house, either; he's just bitter.

JULIAN: About what?

EVELYN: I don't know. Life.

[Pause]

JULIAN: You really should go to sleep. It's the middle of the night.

EVELYN: I know.

[EVELYN throws a pillow angrily, and buries her way under the duvet]

[There is a long pause]

[The ticking clock is ever so loud]

EVELYN: We met in the middle of the night, do you remember?

JULIAN [yawning]: Did we?

EVELYN: Yes. It was at a house party.

JULIAN: I thought we met at the supermarket.

EVELYN: No, it was definitely a house party.

JULIAN: Whose house party?

EVELYN: Caitlin's.

JULIAN: I don't know anyone called Caitlin.

EVELYN: You did, back then.

JULIAN: Back when?

EVELYN: Back when we met . . . Keep up!

JULIAN: Keep up with the past? I don't remember.

EVELYN: You don't remember our beginning?

JULIAN: Apparently not.

EVELYN: Julian! You're so frustrating. In the beginning, there was a house. And there was a party. It was twenty years ago, and it was the end of our first term of university.

Well, it was a flat, rather than a house, really, but we'd sort of sprawled out all over the stairwell so we were taking up most of the building. The neighbours weren't all too impressed. I think they called the police on us at one point.

JULIAN: We should work on our relationship with our neighbours.

EVELYN: Ha! Anyway. It was Caitlin's birthday, or perhaps it was her sister's birthday. It was someone's birthday, anyway. Caitlin was mad about Charlotte Bronte. Like, I think she actually wanted to *be* her. She'd kick up a fuss when we were asked to read anything written after the 1890s because she said that it shouldn't have been invented yet. Caitlin was of another time, and she was having a party where she wanted us all to dress up like it was the 1800s, only hardly anyone did. I remember her sitting in a white dress in the middle of the kitchen surrounded by empty vodka bottles like Miss Havisham or something. One strike of a match and she'd have been alight.

JULIAN: And what were *you* wearing?

EVELYN: I was wearing a black dress, with ruffles.

JULIAN: Ruffles?

EVELYN: I think I got my centuries mixed up. Time's a confusing thing. But I felt sorry for Caitlin.

JULIAN: In the beginning, there was a girl in another time who was transported to a future time and she was miserable.

EVELYN: Exactly. Anyway. There wasn't really anyone at

the party that I liked. I'd got there late, and everyone was pretty much out of it. So, I was just about to leave, when I saw the stairwell up to the roof, and up I went. And then, because that's how things always go – and then, there you were.

JULIAN: I was there?

EVELYN: Yes. You were sitting on the roof. You were by yourself, drinking wine, wearing black trousers and a shirt and a monocle, because you said it was the only thing you could find to make yourself look different. It made one of your eyes look ridiculously large, and I couldn't help laughing.

JULIAN: Sounds about right.

EVELYN: What?

JULIAN: That the first thing you'd do was mock me.

EVELYN: Very funny. [Pause] And *you* did look very funny, you must admit.

JULIAN: I can't admit. I don't remember.

EVELYN: How can you not remember? It was our beginning. On the roof of Caitlin's house. I said that I was a girl who'd stepped out from the future, and that I'd come to tell you that the party downstairs was awful, just so you'd be forewarned.

JULIAN: And I said that it wasn't a forewarning, because I already knew that, which is why I was on the roof in the first place.

EVELYN: So you *do* remember!

JULIAN: No. I'm just guessing. Because you said that I was by myself, on the roof, drinking wine.

EVELYN: Well, that's exactly what you did say. You said that you knew the party was terrible but that it was calm up in the open, so you thought you'd sit there for a while. You handed me the wine bottle, and told me to take a seat, and I did. There were pigeon nests further along, and the occasional puddle. It wasn't flat, either, the roof. It sloped down, like it was about to fall off.

JULIAN: Roofs do tend to slope, you know.

EVELYN: I know that.

JULIAN: Sounds like a stupid thing to be doing, really, climbing a roof like that in the dark, drunk.

EVELYN: Yeah, well, it's the kind of thing we did back then. And, anyway, you went there first.

JULIAN: That's true.

EVELYN: So. We sat, in the wet, near the birds' nests, slugging wine out of a bottle in this new rooftop world of ours. Wine that probably didn't even belong to us, and we looked out across the city. There was a park on the other side of the street, past the terraced houses, leading up to the university. Rows of trees along the paths. So many of them, lined up. Like they could uproot themselves and walk. It was dark, but not pitch black because of all the streetlights. The sky was orange, really orange. Like it was on fire. And I said,

'The sky looks like it's on fire.' And you said, 'I know. I hope the trees don't burn.' And we sat there, watching the sun rise. And I thought: I like you. I like you a lot.

[Pause]

JULIAN: I do remember the orange.

EVELYN: You do?

JULIAN: Yeah, I do. Not an orange light, though. *Oranges.* I remember oranges.

EVELYN: What, the fruit?

JULIAN: Yes, the fruit. I don't remember the roof, or the wine, or the monocle. I remember our beginning being in a supermarket.

EVELYN: I hate supermarkets. Why would I have met you in a supermarket?

JULIAN: Don't bash our beginning, Evelyn. We met in the fruit aisle.

EVELYN [laughing]: No we didn't!

JULIAN: Yes, we did. I was hungover, and you were hungover. It was a Sunday afternoon, and we'd only just woken up. Or, I assumed you'd only just woken up. It certainly looked that way.

EVELYN: Charming.

JULIAN: And I was practically sleepwalking. I'd been writing an essay the night before, and I'd decided to drink whisky to make the essay writing easier, only that didn't work. It just meant that the essay took longer to write.

EVELYN: What was the essay on?

JULIAN: M.W.I.

EVELYN: What's that?

JULIAN: The Many Worlds Interpretation. Where every time you make a decision, the other options you didn't choose play out somewhere. Somewhere else. In some other world. So, somewhere there's a you who didn't go up onto the roof. There's a Caitlin who wasn't sitting by herself. And there's also a me who didn't drink whisky whilst essay-writing, and so wasn't hungover, and therefore didn't feel the need to go and get orange juice and bacon and bread to try and make myself feel better. Anyway. On that particular day, in that particular beginning, in that particular world, I *was* hungover. And so were you, I think. And we were both in a supermarket. You were filling a basket with oranges. Only oranges, nothing else, and people were staring at you.

EVELYN: It's not nice to stare.

JULIAN: Well, I was staring, too. You were piling about a dozen or so into a basket. There wasn't any orange juice left, because the supermarket got deliveries on Mondays so most of the shelves were empty. So, I thought, 'Hey, I'll just buy oranges and make the juice myself.' Only you were hogging all the oranges.

EVELYN: You were going to make orange juice yourself, when you were hungover? Did you even own a juicer as a student?

JULIAN: I wasn't exactly thinking straight.

EVELYN: I guess not.

JULIAN: So, anyway, I went over to you and said: 'I'd like some oranges, too, please.' And you just looked at me, like I'd said something stupid, and you said, 'Go ahead. It's a free country.' And I felt like saying that it isn't a free country, because all decisions are predetermined and all of them happen, all of the time, just in different places in different worlds. But I couldn't say that.

EVELYN: You mean, you *chose* not to say that.

JULIAN: Well, I . . .

EVELYN: So, that's free will right there. You chose not to say those things to me.

JULIAN: Another me, somewhere else, did say those things to you, though.

EVELYN: Yeah, and another me probably looked at you in disdain and walked off and never saw you again.

JULIAN: Well, I didn't say anything back, and you left four oranges in the box, and I picked them up and put them in my basket, and then I followed you to the till.

'What are you going to do with all of those oranges?' I asked you.

'I'm building a sculpture with them,' you said. 'It's an art project.'

'You're building a sculpture with oranges? A sculpture of what?'

'The sun,' you said. 'A huge burning star. I'm going to use a glue gun. It might not work.'

'Won't the art . . . decay?'

'That's life,' you said. 'Things are born. And then they die.'

EVELYN: I don't remember any of this.

JULIAN: Well, that's what you said. That your art class was doing a project on the beginning of the world. Something pretentious about creating things about creation. And I said, that's a coincidence, and I told you about my essay. About beginnings and endings and the possibility of other worlds.

EVELYN: And that was our beginning?

JULIAN: It was one of our beginnings. Somewhere. Somehow.

EVELYN: Look at us, beginning and ending all over the place.

[Pause]

EVELYN: I miss you, Julian.

JULIAN: I know. What about your beloved tree? How do you think that began?

EVELYN: I like to think it began accidentally. Just by chance. A stray seed on the wind that burrowed its way into the soil.

JULIAN: Or was planted by a king, long ago.

EVELYN: Or perhaps just an ordinary person.

JULIAN: Maybe a you in another world planted it, and sent it here.

EVELYN [laughing]: A tree travelling through time and space?

JULIAN: Yeah. Why not?

EVELYN: I can think of many logical reasons why not.

JULIAN: I thought we weren't supposed to be using logic tonight.

EVELYN: That's true.

[The clock ticks loudly. Birds begin to sing outside]

JULIAN: If they cut our tree down, it'll still exist somewhere else, you know.

EVELYN [smiling]: I suppose that's true.

[Pause]

JULIAN: Evelyn?

EVELYN: Yeah?

JULIAN: What about our ending?

EVELYN: I don't like to think about it.

JULIAN: No. Me neither.

[Pause]

JULIAN: I didn't want to leave, you know.

EVELYN: I know.

[Orange light trickles into the room. The sun is rising]

EVELYN: You're here now, though, right?

JULIAN: Now?

EVELYN: Yeah, right now.

JULIAN: Sure. I'm here. Go to sleep.

Pebbles

The shortest war in history was between the United Kingdom and Zanzibar in 1896.

It lasted thirty-eight minutes.

We read a book about Northern Ireland at school. A novel about a boy from one side and a girl from the other. We had one of those teachers who spoke like Shakespeare. Everything she said was for dramatic effect. I remember giggling into my sleeve when she spat out rude words.

I thought I knew everything about the war. About religious fighting with bricks and fists and falling in love with girls on the other side. It was twenty years ago. I was young.

'What the hell are they complaining about? It's romantic,' I said, as we walked home along the cliff tops. 'War's like this whole fucking romantic thing. Romeo and Juliet. Those petrol bombs, you know. Burning love.'

'It's like football.' George swiped a tongue on a roll-up, nearly dropping it. 'We're all sport.' And he pointed his finger to the side of his temple and mimicked pulling a trigger. 'Bang, said the gun,' he said.

'But guns don't talk,' I said, squinting at the smoke.

'Neither do the dead,' he said. Then he grinned like he was mad.

We walked past some kids sitting in trees, making parachutes out of plastic bags. They tied them to 2B pencils and let them drop, slowly, to the ground.

During World War I, British tanks were categorised as 'male' or 'female'. Male tanks had cannons. Female tanks had machine guns.

In the eighties, when I was young, the threat was petrol bombs. Northern Ireland was only a ferry ride away. And we heard about the IRA and raging politicians and other snippets of conversations on the news. And then there was talk of nuclear power, and how damaging was that, exactly? And what was the world coming to? And *please* could someone protect the children? We played a game called Fireball at school, where you'd throw a rubber ball, hard, across the playground and someone on the other team had to catch it. It hurt like hell. The person catching it had to pretend that it didn't. They had to stand there and take it. As though it didn't burn.

In the 1400s, during the Spanish Inquisition, a form of torture similar to water-boarding called *toca* was invented.

Victims were forced to ingest water from a jar poured over their faces, until they felt as though they were drowning (because they were).

I liked to think I knew how it was over there, in Belfast. I lay awake one night, thinking about it. Somewhere, there was a girl, one I was deeply in love with, and she had bright-red hair. Her name was something wonderful, and she was the sister of the leader of a local gang. Throwing stones in the name of God. A shared God. A different God. A God from over the other side of town. She was marvellous. She used to kiss boys and girls for cigarettes. I knew that I could find her on the corner of a street, sharpening pebbles, putting them in her pocket. I knew that she would give me one of those pebbles, press it into the palm of my hand until the sharp edges cut me, as she kissed me behind the bike sheds and we forgot about the world, and she said it was all going to be OK – somehow – in the end. It's because war's romantic, I thought. And dangerous. It's a red-haired girl, kissing another girl, me, under a streetlight, with no one caring because there's a whole damn war on, and they care more about which side you're on, instead of what gender you are and who the hell you're kissing. That's what I imagined, you see. That's what I thought.

*

Did you know at least ninety-two nuclear weapons have been lost at sea?

You said: 'Let's go to Brighton Pride and see how it's changed.'

I had nothing to compare it to; I'd never been. You had to work late the night before, so I looked it all up on the Internet – all the pictures, all the stories. When you got back, I spent the night in bed telling you about the first Brighton Pride, in 1992. I dreamed of all the tents, wondering how many people it took to put them up. Joke: how many lesbians does it take to build a tent? And then I woke myself up because I couldn't think of an answer and suddenly I couldn't breathe, stuck under the sheets. Like when they used to say you should bury your head in a plastic bag if a country declares nuclear war. Take deep breaths and let the world float away. 'They'll blow our atoms out our ears,' my granddad used to tell me, cursing the modern world. 'In the future,' he said, 'I bet the government'll weed out plastic bags, too. And how the hell will we save ourselves then?'

We got a train from London Bridge and the platform was packed, the carriage stuffy, one from a smaller company, with chairs that smelled of tobacco and sweat. We just managed to fit on the corner of one seat, opposite a family.

Suitcases scattered all around their feet. The mother of the children, one girl and one boy, looked around at the tight clothes, the placards and the feathers.

A group of twenty-somethings started singing 'Summer Holiday'.

'Mum, why are those men dressed like cowboys?'

'It looks as though they're going to a party,' she replied, raising an eyebrow at those who looked on.

You collapsed with the giggles and sang along with the rest.

I closed my eyes but started picturing falling-down tents.

I could feel my pulse in my throat.

I took a deep breath.

I once saw an art installation called *One Hundred and Eight*. It's by Nils Volker and consists of one hundred and eight plastic bags. These bags are lined along a wall and are inflated and deflated by a machine. They look like jellyfish lungs and sound like the wind.

It's like the exhibition is alive. Like it's whispering in your ear.

You offered me a crisp and it tasted like the sea.

At Gatwick, all the cowboys jumped off the train to let the family get by. They carried their suitcases for them, up over their heads, and tipped their hats. You told me you'd always wanted to be a cowgirl.

At Brighton, we walked down towards the beach. The street lamps were covered in rainbow bunting. You disappeared for a minute and came back with two ice creams in one hand, and a pink cowboy hat covered with tacky plastic jewels.

'Howdy,' you said, and slipped it over my head.

The strap met under my chin, and scratched my skin when I turned from side to side. We marched towards the Royal Pavilion at Preston Park. The website said it had been built for George IV, mocked as a carnival sideshow, transformed into a palace. It announced itself loudly. A place within a place.

'You know, there was a fire here, twenty years ago,' I said.

You took my hand.

As we turned the corner, I saw them. The police first, in their yellow fluorescent jackets looking bored beyond belief. There must have been ten of them, forming a neon circle around a dozen people holding signs.

'You've got to be joking,' and I heard you laugh. 'I thought they'd do better than that.'

The last time you were here, there had been so many angry people lining the streets, but now the police outnumbered the protesters. One man holding a sign that said

'God **Abhors** **You**' threw an empty water bottle in our direction. The police didn't move.

'God pities your choices!' a lady shouted as we walked past.

'Oh *please*,' you said under your breath. 'She sounds like my mother . . . It isn't her, is it?'

I tried to grin. 'Shouldn't we . . . shouldn't we say something back?'

'Are you kidding? They won't listen.'

'But why do they care?'

'Why do you?'

I faltered.

'Come on.' You tugged my hand and dragged me onto the grass verge. You took the cowboy hat off my head and put it on yours instead. 'For goodness' sake, let's have some fun.'

One out of every two casualties of war is a civilian caught in the crossfire.

Later that night, after we'd danced under naked light bulbs and laughed ourselves silly, we weaved our way through the streets back to the beach, through Victoria Gardens with hedges cut into domes. The sun was setting at the end of the pier, a wooden walkway like an aisle reaching out into the water, and you went to buy us chips.

I pulled my sandals off and flopped down onto the pebbled beach. The heels had been cutting into my skin where my feet had swollen in the heat. I let my feet slide under the loose stones, let myself imagine that I was sinking. In the distance I could see you, pick you out from the pink cowboy hat that clashed with your red hair. You were queuing outside a kebab house. I raised my arms in the air, pretending I was falling under, that you'd have to rush over and save me, but you were looking in the other direction. I found myself laughing: I could fall right under all this, I thought to myself, my toenails catching on the edges of stray shells. I could tumble under this and never be found. It would be like a rock slide, fighting gravity, punching at the air, fighting, fighting. Buried alive.

In 2011, after a tsunami flooded the Fukushima power station in Japan, over two hundred pensioners, calling themselves The Skilled Veterans Corps, volunteered to go and live at the power station and work to cool the reactors. They wanted to save the younger workers from radiation exposure and cancer. It was organised by a man called Mr Yamada, a retired engineer, who was seventy-two. Some people called them the Kamikaze Corps.

Once, when I was walking through town, I said I wanted to do a survey. I said that I bet we could go up to people in the streets and ask them if there's a war going on and that ninety per cent of them would say no. I bet that they would look at me strangely, and hurry off down the street.

By the age of sixteen, an American child has seen, on average, 18,000 murders on television.

I pulled myself out from under the stones and stared at the waves.

You weren't back yet.

I walked into the sea with all my clothes on.

I thought it would be dramatic. I imagined waves coming up to meet me and me shouting in their face, but I was so aware of myself that I just felt stupid and embarrassed and, anyway, the water was cold. I could tell that there were some people watching me from the pier. I could see a few teenagers laughing in the crowd.

I stepped forward and stumbled head first into the next wave. Everything went silent. You see, if you put your head underwater then everything stops existing. Words are no longer words, but drawn-out sounds in plastic bags. It makes your eyes bulge and your chest hurt. It is wonderful and intoxicating and pulls your hair in all directions. It is beautiful and terrifying: so big that not being able to see the edges of it makes you sick, forcing you upwards to breathe. The sea pushes you back up; it saves you. I gasped, dragging myself to my feet, my clothes completely drenched.

'What the hell are you doing?'

I turned.

There you were. You'd left the chips on the edge of the beach and waded in, up to your knees. The cowboy hat had fallen off the back of your head, the strap cutting into your neck. I had a desperate urge to cut it free.

'Did you know that war's like this whole fucking romantic thing?' I said, starting to shiver.

'What?'

'Did you know that? I read it in a book once.'

Waves were hitting the backs of my legs.

'But . . . War's bullshit,' you said. 'It's not romantic at all.'

Your hair was plastered to one side of your face. I could hear people shouting. I bent down and picked up a pebble, shimmering in the light.

I stepped forward and gave it to you, pressed it hard into your palm.

And then I kissed you and, for that second, just for that one moment, the whole world and all its bullshit completely disappeared.

Aunt Libby's Coffin Hotel

EXTRAORDINARY ANKAA:
ANGEL OF DEATH

Desperate to communicate with deceased loved ones?

Looking for answers about mortality?

Dare to spend an evening toying with death?

Spend a night at Libitina Dart's Coffin Hotel, and meet Ankaa, Angel of Death.

Just thirteen years old, this changeling has untold wisdom collected from years spent in Hades.

So named because she is anchored to the underworld, yet tied to the night-time sky, Ankaa is a child stuck between heaven and hell.

A personification of Purgatory.

A dark fairy trapped in time.

DON'T MISS THIS ONCE-IN-A-LIFETIME DEATH EXPERIENCE.*

*Visitors are encouraged to visit multiple times.

Each visit requires payment in full. See website for details.

It's all a bit much.

I shove the fliers through the letterboxes of the bungalows on Sunshine Place, and hover at the street sign pointing towards St Bernadette's.

'Make sure you hit up the old people's home!' my aunt had yelled that morning, as I pulled my bike out from the bushes. 'And the hospital! Don't forget the hospital!'

I remember Mrs Turner and her husband. I remember Eric and his son. I glance up at the sign once more, then push off in the opposite direction. Screw that. Cerberus barks appreciatively and runs along beside me, occasionally stopping to assault a garden gnome. He's not supposed to be out with me on the mainland, but it's still early and no one's out. We reach the water before sunrise, and I tie the remaining fliers to a stone. Cerberus looks at me, head tilted.

'It'd break your teeth,' I grin. 'This one's not for you.'

I pull my arm back, bend my knees, and throw it out into the lake.

It makes a satisfying *plop*. The edges of the fliers curl and sag, then disappear out of sight.

By the time I row back to the island, I have to sprint to get to our guests in time for the alarm. As I run, I take a moment to knock each doll head on the way, for luck; they swing from the willow branches, covered in dew.

'Death makes a person hungry, Ankaa,' Aunt Libby reminds me most mornings. 'That's why we charge extra for bacon and jam.'

Smoke is billowing out from the kitchen window, and I can hear her banging pots and pans. Occasionally, she swears at the microwave.

'Cerberus!' He bounds over and I pull his costume out of my bag. He sees it and snorts. 'I know,' I coax, pulling it over his head and slipping his legs through the holes. It's not easy dressing an Irish Wolfhound.

'You look . . . radiant,' I trail off.

He scowls, knowing better.

'Time to rise and shine, Mr Henderson' I tap the top of his coffin and begin to pull out the nails. I have to stand on a chair to do it. 'Wakey, wakey!'

Before I have the last nail out properly, Mr Henderson pushes the lid from the inside and I almost fall over backwards. He sits bolt upright, his suit dishevelled, clutching his chest and gasping for air.

'Oh, I'm alive!' he cries, blinking in the sudden light. 'I'm alive! Yes? Really alive?'

He reaches over and yanks me into an embrace. The chair totters beneath me.

'There, there, Mr Henderson.' I gingerly pat his sweaty head. 'Welcome back to the world.'

'I saw her, you know.' Mr Henderson lets go of me but his hands are still shaking. 'I saw her, all of her. Blurry, she was, and there was a lot of light. They say that about the afterlife, don't they? Lots of light. Like stars. Glowing, and stuff.' He glances up at the light bulbs. 'And she was talking about catching the 63 bus to the seaside, she was. We used to do that, sometimes, on our anniversary, I told you that. The 63 bus.' He looks off into the distance, hair poking out in all directions. 'I heard the bus, and the sea, too, I swear it.'

'That's great.'

There's a muffled shout from a mahogany coffin across the room. 'You know, some of us like a quiet start to the morning!'

'Don't mind Trevor, Mr Henderson.' I help him climb out of his coffin. 'Would you like to shower now, or after breakfast?'

He blinks, looking down at himself, as though surprised to see his body there. 'Oh, afterwards, afterwards.'

'Lovely. Breakfast is just through the double doors, down the corridor on the right.'

Mr Henderson tries and fails to walk in a straight line. After a few stumbling steps, he disappears out the door. Trevor starts banging furiously from inside his coffin.

'All right, all right. I thought you said you like quiet in the mornings!' I rush over to pull the nails out of the lid.

'I do,' he pouts, sitting up. He stretches his arms so high his shoulders click. 'But I don't want to bloody suffocate while I wait.'

'I wasn't that late.'

'You were.'

'I was not.'

'I thought of thirty more ways I don't want to die, just lying there, and it's awfully difficult to write them down in the dark.'

'I bet.'

'You should put a light bulb inside. Add some accessories. Like when they used to put bells inside coffins, in case anyone was buried alive.'

'Wouldn't a light bulb ruin the ambience?'

'It might be cosy.'

'It might also set the coffin on fire.'

'Oh, true!' Trevor pulls a notebook from his breast pocket and scribbles down *Way I Don't Want to Die #1584:*

Trapped in blazing coffin. 'I don't want that, Ankaa; you're quite right.'

'Here's your extra bacon, Mr Henderson.'

'Thank you, Libitina.'

'Please, call me Libby.' She shimmies into her chair at the head of the table.

'Well, thank you Libby.' He raises his glass of orange juice to her, and then to me. 'Last night was just a phenomenal experience.'

'I'm glad to hear it.'

'And I must ask.' Mr Henderson squints, peering over at the frosted glass in the kitchen door. 'Where *did* you find that three-headed dog?'

Cerberus whines, pawing at the glass.

'Oh, it's a fascinating story, Mr Henderson,' Aunt Libby beams. 'Do eat up, there's plenty more where that came from. You see, at the end of every summer, Ankaa and I leave the Coffin Hotel for two weeks. Breaks my heart to do it, you understand, but it's important to spread the word about us to people out there, like you, who truly need us.'

She pauses for a second to frown at Trevor, who is shovelling baked beans into his mouth as though he's never seen food before.

'We have a mobile version of the hotel, parked just round the back. It's a converted RV, with ten coffins, quite comfortable. Plenty of choice between the wood, and linings, Mr Henderson. We didn't want to cut any corners; just because we're travelling doesn't mean the customers should miss out on quality. We tend to set off at the end of September, just when the autumn's coming. It's a beautiful time of year to drive around the country, just beautiful.'

Mr Henderson nods in agreement, egg yolk caught in his moustache.

'I knew you'd agree, a fine man like you.' She sips her coffee. 'So, we spend about two weeks driving around the neighbouring towns, telling everyone we meet about our dear little Ankaa and her extraordinary talents. We're fully booked every night, with those who want to rent the coffins and experience a night of death. Those who do turn up when we have no room at the inn, so to speak, Mr Henderson, tend to visit our website, and often travel across to visit the hotel during the coming year.'

'And, er, you found the dog during one of those trips, is that it?'

'Very perceptive of you, very perceptive.' She pours him another cup of tea. 'You see, your sixth sense has been awakened after only one night in our hotel. We did find Cerberus while we were out travelling. Sometimes we team up with a company run by my second cousin, you see, perhaps you've heard of him, Mr Henderson? He runs Christopher's Cabinet of Curiosities, not to be confused with Foley's Freaks; Mr

Foley is not a nice man, Mr Henderson, I'm sure you've seen the reviews. He displays people pretending that they are magical or mystical, sometimes well-known mythological creatures, but really, they're all wearing costumes. Costumes! Can you imagine, Mr Henderson? It's a disgrace!'

'Terrible, terrible.'

Cerberus growls.

'I knew you'd understand. My cousin, on the other hand, does no such thing. He has travelled the world collecting true human oddities, and mythological creatures. He found Cerberus's mother at Cape Matapan, already pregnant, and allowed us to keep one of the litter. His Cabinet of Curiosities really is something to behold, Mr Henderson. I can give you his contact information if you'd like to look him up; we make sure to exchange details with our customers, considering we both dabble with the Unknown. But, as I was saying, he has all manner of wonderful creatures in his care – chimeras, nymphs, sea-goats, sirens. He even had a werewolf for a while, which gave me a bit of a turn, though he turned out to be a true gentleman, actually. Which reminds me that one shouldn't believe everything one reads, Mr Henderson. History can be very cruel about those who are different. Take Ankaa, for example. She may be a death fairy in human form, but does that mean she should be treated as a second-class citizen? Absolutely not.'

All three of them turn to stare at me.

Cerberus starts barking.

'Can we let him in?' Mr Henderson makes a move to stand up. 'I'd love to see him up close.'

'Best not, Mr Henderson.' Aunt Libby rests her hand on his arm. 'As much as we love our dear Cerberus, he is quite vicious. He's a descendant of the underworld, after all. He's been through a lot. He's had to learn to be tough. He's trusting with Ankaa, of course, because she knew his ancestor, from her time before birth, so she's like a kindred spirit to him, really. But everyone else should stay well clear and just admire him from afar.'

'Oh, of course,' Mr Henderson sits back down. 'Don't want to antagonise the beast. Fascinating stuff, though. So, er, Ankaa. If you don't mind me asking. What was it like in the underworld?'

'Oh, it was very . . . dark,' I offer.

Aunt Libby tries to kick me under the table but gets Trevor by mistake.

'Oh, I am sorry, Trevor. Talk of the underworld makes me jumpy. Let me give you some more beans. Do go on, Ankaa.'

'It's all very hazy, really,' I say. 'Sometimes it was so hot I felt my skin would melt. Sometimes it was freezing. I wasn't quite formed. I was just a young fairy. But they say that adult fairies trapped in the world of the dead want to help their young escape. They use magic to implant them in the wombs of humans so they can grow up in this world, instead. It's not easy to come across from the world of the dead, though. A sacrifice has to be made.'

'Which is why my sister died, Mr Henderson,' Aunt Libby chimes in. 'During childbirth. We didn't know the father of the baby, she wouldn't tell us anything about it, rest her soul, but we suspect perhaps he was Death in disguise.'

'Goodness!'

'Yes, it was all rather distressing, Mr Henderson. She just turned up at my house one day. Eight months pregnant, and distraught. She gave birth to Ankaa, here. On the very table we're eating at.'

Mr Henderson pales.

'And when she gave birth to Ankaa, she passed away. Just like that. Well, not "just like that", there was a lot of blood, of course; it took her a while to die. But her passing must have formed a pathway to the afterlife, you see, and Ankaa was able to descend and come to life in the form of her child. Some sort of changeling, Mr Henderson. And, even though she technically killed my sister, what could I do? I couldn't throw her out into the wilderness, it's not in my nature. I had to take care of her. I'm not one to judge hastily, you see. And she's got a good soul, really, our Ankaa. She hasn't killed anyone else. She's more of a keeper of death, if you will. And that's why we've set up our Coffin Hotel here because, ever since she was born, the boundaries between life and death seem so much weaker on this island. As I'm sure you will have experienced last night.'

'Yes, indeed.' Mr Henderson pats his moustache with a napkin. 'It is a remarkable place you have here, Libitina.'

'Thank you. We take great pride in what we do,' she beams. 'And now that you've finished breakfast, perhaps you'd like a tour of the funeral parlour?'

'That would be lovely.' He scrapes his chair back. 'Is there a Mr Dart who helps run the business?'

'He passed away fifteen years ago.' Aunt Libby clasps her chest, a well-practised gesture.

'Oh, I am sorry.'

'Thank you. It's just the two of us here now. And Zima.'

'Who's Zima?'

'She runs the hotel for us when we go on tour, so we don't have to close. It's very important that we're always here for those who need us, Mr Henderson. We can't offer our whole range of services with Ankaa absent, of course, but we can offer the basics. Zima's not here at the moment so you won't be able to meet her. She's a lovely girl, if a little odd. Just turned eighteen. Descended from a family of vampires, and suffers from insomnia. Vegetarian, though, which is a comfort. It's an ideal end-of-summer job for her; she loves it, and we can go off in the RV knowing that this place is in safe hands, which is a relief. It's apt that three women run the place, Mr Henderson.'

'How so?'

'Well, I like to think of us as the modern-day Fates. Women may be lots of things, but one of those things is that we are responsible for death and it's something we needn't shy away from, Mr Henderson. Nothing to be ashamed of. Running this hotel is our way of giving back, as it were – compensation for letting death out into the world. I'm sure Ankaa can tell you more about that, when she shows you around the island, later. We've got lots of wonderful creatures here, hiding out in the woods. Ankaa's pets. They tend not to come out until dusk, so let me give you a tour of the funeral parlour as suggested, then we can have a chat, sort out your accounts and Ankaa can take it from there.'

'Sounds great.'

'Excellent. Are you going to take Trevor back to the mainland, Ankaa?' Aunt Libby folds her napkin firmly. 'We don't want him to be late for work.'

It takes twenty minutes to row across the lake.

Trevor clings to the side and keeps his eyes shut the whole way.

'You know, this is your sixtieth time,' I say, avoiding a jagged rock. 'And I haven't sent you flying into the water, yet.'

'Shhh,' he breathes in through his nose and out through his mouth.

'Well, I think you're doing a good job,' I coax. 'Do you think your stay is helping?'

'My therapist thinks so.' He doesn't open his eyes but recites: 'To confront death is to belittle death, is to come to terms with death, is to live.'

'You should get that printed on a T-shirt.'

The corners of his mouth curve upwards.

He tries to press money into my hand when we reach the shore but I refuse to take it.

'You can have this one for free,' I say. 'You've been staying with us long enough. Consider it a "buy fifty-nine, get one free" type thing.'

He looks puzzled, trying to work out if I'm tricking him. 'No, it's fine.' He throws the money into the bottom of the boat. 'Don't want to cheat death.'

'I thought that was exactly what you were trying to do!' I call after him as he wanders off. He raises a hand in farewell. 'See you at six!' I use an oar to push off the bank, the mist starting to clear from the surface of the water.

Back home, I find Cerberus and together we head to the woodshed, to collect extra dolls. Aunt Libby's voice floats out from inside the funeral parlour.

'You see, Mr Henderson, we can offer you any type of coffin you like. Our most sought-after are the walnut and mahogany, though we can also offer bespoke sculpture coffins, and we have these remarkable caskets made out of crushed oyster shells shipped over from Taiwan.'

'I read online about eco-friendly coffins, do you have any of those?'

'Oh, Mr Henderson, that's just a fad and we pay no heed to fashion here. Cheap tat, as I'm sure you agree. Now, let me show you our coffins lined with marble – walk this way . . .'

We only have one bin-liner full of dolls left. I make a mental note to buy more, pocket a mini toolkit and drag the bag out into the daylight. I tip the dolls onto the soil. Some already have limbs missing, a few with empty eye sockets and balding scalps. I help the others along by fishing out a screwdriver and begin scraping at their plastic skin. Cerberus hunts for frogs while I work.

We started hanging dolls around the island just over a year ago, after Aunt Libby found Isla de las Muñecas online. A floating garden, surrounded by canals, just south of Mexico City, covered with thousands and thousands of dolls. They hang from trees and washing lines, fences and signposts. Decapitated heads impaled on sticks, their stuffing tumbling to the ground.

'They say a young girl died there, Ankaa,' Aunt Libby told me, her face lit up by the blue computer screen. 'They say that the dolls are possessed by her spirit. They whisper to people across the water, and lure them in.'

Don Julian Santana Barrera used to be the caretaker of

the island. He said he found a girl in the canal who had drowned there and, two weeks later, discovered a floating doll in exactly the same spot. Thinking the doll was a message from the dead girl, he started hanging them all over the island to summon her spirit. To appease her ghost. He said the dolls moved and spoke to him. That they whispered thanks and blessings and magic.

Don Julian collected the dolls for fifty years, and was then discovered drowned, in exactly the same spot that the girl had drowned before him. These days the island is a tourist attraction, and people travel from far and wide to view the ant-infested dolls, leaving figurines of their own.

'Perhaps dolls will encourage people to visit us, too, Ankaa,' Aunt Libby said. 'Best order a hundred or so on eBay, and hang them around the place, like Christmas lights. You can tell visitors they're your little friends.'

I rip off one of the doll heads and throw it into the lake. Cerberus bounds after it, enthusiastically, and brings it back to me covered in teeth marks.

I spend the afternoon working on our Krasue puppets, Moroaica lights and Seven Whistles tapes. I cup my hands over my mouth and make moaning noises, the occasional shriek. I record the sounds in a cave for maximum echo. It takes a while to get it right, as Cerberus keeps howling in the background, thinking it's a game he can join in.

At six, I collect Trevor from the mainland, and as the sun begins to set, Aunt Libby brings Mr Henderson out into the graveyard.

'I'm delighted to say Mr Henderson has picked his coffin, Ankaa, and has decided to register with us, so that we can perform his funeral when the time comes, though of course we hope that won't be any time soon.' She pats his shoulder. 'And, until that time, he's going to be visiting us once a month, staying for a couple of days at a time, to prepare himself for what's to come.'

'Indeed.' Mr Henderson wraps a tartan scarf around his neck. 'It's good to know I'm in safe hands here.'

'He'd love to have a tour of the island,' Aunt Libby continues. 'So, why don't you show him, while I put dinner on?'

We take the stone path around the side of the hotel, into the trees. Cerberus barks from the kitchen, forbidden to follow.

'Do we need torches?' Mr Henderson asks. 'It'll be completely dark soon.'

'Don't worry, I know my way around.'

He hesitates for a second, before hurrying to catch up.

'Will Trevor be joining us?'

'No, he's done the tour many times before.'

'Has he been here a long time, then?'

'A couple of weeks.' I head purposefully into the

undergrowth without waiting for him to follow. 'Trevor lives in the neighbouring village. He has a chronic fear of dying and his therapist recommended he do something to confront it. That's why he's staying here.'

'Interesting.' Mr Henderson almost trips over a fallen tree. 'Ankaa, why are the door frames of the hotel painted black?'

'Oh, we brush tar on them, to stop the Keres getting in.'

'What are Keres?'

'Female death spirits. I've spied some in the woods a few times. Descendants of those who escaped Pandora's Box. Whilst they have their uses, they also have a fetish for infecting the living with disease. So, we like to keep our distance. We certainly don't want to invite them in for a cup of tea.'

'No.' Mr Henderson looks ahead nervously.

'You're safe with me, don't worry. They won't come close, if I'm by your side.' I run my fingers along one of the rag dolls on a nearby tree. 'You see, some say Pandora was the first woman to walk the earth, Mr Henderson. She was hammered into existence by Hephaestus, and given a golden diadem made of animals and sea creatures. Athena gave her a silver dress and Hermes gave her a silver tongue.

'Pandora was designed by the gods to be a plague on men and, in the house of Epimetheus, she found a gift from those gods. It was a beautiful jar, the same size as herself, and it whispered across the room. *Come closer, look inside.*

'And because Pandora had been programmed with greed, and because Aphrodite had given her desire, she reached over and opened the jar. A scream filled the room and darkness fell everywhere. The evils of the world flooded out into the sky. Death, and misery, and every kind of sin.

'All that was left in the jar was a wisp of white smoke. Pandora slammed the lid back down to try and keep it inside. The smoke fluttered and it spluttered. It moved just like a bird. *Hope . . .* it whispered. *Hope . . .* Zeus smiled, and Pandora cried.'

Mr Henderson shivers, pulling a hat from his coat pocket.

'It's all very . . . intriguing,' he says. 'You certainly know your stuff.'

'It's in my genes,' I shrug. 'If you look into the distance here, Mr Henderson, you might be able to see the lights of the Moroaica.'

'Where?'

I point over to our left where, far off, there are blinking red lights. In the dark, they look as though they are floating of their own accord. Really, they are left-over Christmas lights we bought in bulk from a hardware store. I attached them to a series of pulleys, so they flicker up and down.

'Moroaica are from Romania, Mr Henderson. They're

women who shapeshift into glowing balls of light. Sometimes they turn into animals, but this is their favourite form. If you saw them as their true selves, you'd see that they have red hair, two hearts and bright-red cheeks. They like to drain the life from plants and animals. Humans, too, if they're feeling extra wicked.'

Mr Henderson watches them, fearfully, a bead of sweat trickling down his forehead.

'I don't mean to offend, Ankaa, but I was always sceptical about all of this.' He gestures into the night. 'It was my wife, Rosemary, who believed in it all. Moroi and vampires and ghosts. She had books and books on superstitions and stories. Real-life accounts from people who claimed to have seen the other side.'

'And what changed your mind?'

'Well, Rosemary always said that, if she died, she'd come back to haunt me just to prove a point,' he laughs weakly. 'She didn't like to lose an argument. And . . . well . . . since she passed, I've started seeing her. Only glimpses, mind you. I see her red scarf at the bus stop. Hear her laugh late at night. The sound of her shoes in the kitchen in the morning as I lie in bed upstairs. Sometimes I smell her perfume so strongly, I swear she's standing right behind me. But when I turn, there's nothing there.'

'What perfume did she wear?'

'I don't remember the name of it, but it smelled of roses.'

'Women have a special relationship with death, Mr Henderson. It doesn't surprise me that she comes back to visit.'

'And do you really believe that women created death?'

'Most cultures around the world have stories that say so, yes.'

'Eve, and so on?'

'Eve. Pandora. Many others. In the Banks Islands of the Coral Sea, it's said men used to live forever. When their skin became wrinkled and creased, they simply discarded it as snakes do, and stepped back into the world smooth, new and innocent.

'But, one day, an old woman discarded her skin in a river, where it floated downstream and caught on a branch. The woman, now looking youthful, skipped back home. But her grandchildren didn't recognise her – they cried and ran away. She searched for them up mountains and in forests, but still they would not come to her. So she returned to the river and pulled her old skin back on. Then her grandchildren came running, but so too did death. After that, no man could live forever. And it was all the woman's fault.'

The red lights in the distance bob and float.

'Now, let me take you to the cave of Seven Whistles. Sometimes you can hear the spirits there, gathering to chant. And keep an eye out for the Krasue. They come over from Southeast Asia: the floating heads of beautiful women, whispering in the dark.'

'One thing I don't understand,' Mr Henderson's hat gets stuck on a branch, and he struggles to pull himself free. 'If your Coffin Hotel allows us to come here and spend a night in the world of the dead. If you cast a spell while we sleep, so we're sent there for a few hours . . . why don't we just die? Do you summon us back?'

'Partly. It's all rather complicated,' I say, vaguely. 'Many people have tried to document the phenomenon. In the Qur'an, for example, it's believed that humans are animated by a self or spirit, called nafs. Nafs represent the soul. During the night, nafs are taken away by Allah to dance in the world of the dead, and those who are destined to survive are sent home again in the morning.'

Mr Henderson stops. 'So, what happens to us is not actually within your control?'

I sense his panic. 'It is and it isn't. Try not to worry. This is something that happens to everyone, every night, when they sleep, regardless of where they are. What happens here is slightly different, slightly heightened. Even I don't understand my powers fully, Mr Henderson. But I promise that we look after you to the best of our ability. It's all covered in the terms and conditions, which you signed yesterday.'

'OK.' He starts walking again. 'I suppose one can't really

expect to have these types of experiences without some form of risk, realistically. But . . . no one has ever died unexpectedly, have they? I mean, whilst staying at your hotel?'

I try not to think of Eric and his panic attack. I try not to think of Mrs Turner's scratch marks on the inside of her coffin.

'No,' I lie smoothly. 'Never.'

'Did you have a good time?' Aunt Libby helps Mr Henderson out of his coat. The hallway smells of chicken and dumplings.

'Oh, very illuminating,' he gasps, his cheeks red from the cold. 'It's started blowing a gale out there, mind you. Out by the cave, I swear I heard Rosemary calling my name on the wind.'

'How wonderful.' Aunt Libby thrusts the coat into my hands and ushers Mr Henderson forward. 'You must be starving, come and eat.'

They disappear into the dining room. I hang back, arms full of tweed and tartan. Through the wall, I hear Trevor telling them about his goals for the rest of the year. How he plans to go bungee jumping, and bareback horse riding.

'And I might even get on a plane,' he says boldly. 'I'm not making any promises. But I might very well do it. I'd like to visit my sister; I haven't seen her in eleven years.'

There's a knock at the front door.

I put Mr Henderson's coat on the floor, and struggle to pull the heavy door open. The wind outside snakes its way past me, whistling in my ears.

'Hello?' I call out, my hair blowing every which way. '. . . Hello?'

There's no one there.

I tiptoe out onto the doorstep and glance around, pulling my cardigan close. I can barely make out the lake, the wind rushing white smoke across the surface, tumbling like broken birds. Everything is dark, bar the red lights of the fake Moroaica, which seem, somehow, closer than before.

I slip back inside.

'Ankaa?' Aunt Libby calls. 'What *are* you doing?'

I slam the door.

'Coming!' I shove Mr Henderson's coat on the rack, along with his scarf, and hurry through for food.

'Did you find out anything more about Rosemary?' Aunt Libby asks, as we clean up after dinner.

'She used to wear a red scarf and wore a perfume that smelled of roses.'

'Excellent. I think we've got some rose-water in the cupboard. You can use that along with the coastal sounds.'

'OK.'

She passes me a tea towel. 'By the way, if he mentions

it, I've promised Mr Henderson that, when he dies, you'll be able to send him to the same part of the afterlife as Rosemary.'

I blink. 'What?'

'Well, he was very concerned, Ankaa, because, as he pointed out, logically, the afterlife must be endless. And he was panicking about getting there and being unable to find her amid the billions of other people.'

'So?'

'So I said that we could fix that for him . . . for a fee.'

I scowl. 'We've never said we could do that before!'

'I know, but the man's rich, what does it matter?'

'He's not rich! He works at the Post Office!'

Cerberus cowers in the corner.

'Look,' she frowns. 'I am doing my best. You know bookings have been low this season. I'm just working with what I've got.'

'But it's not fair . . .'

'People come here looking for answers, Ankaa. They come here looking for answers, and we tell them what they want to hear.'

'Yes, but—'

'We are helping them, remember that.' She wrenches the cupboard door open and hunts around for rose-water. 'They are lost and we are helping. OK? Just do as I say.'

*

Trevor's in pyjamas, Mr Henderson's in a suit.

'It was Rosemary's favourite,' he says, when I ask if he wants to change into something a little more comfortable. 'I always wore it for our anniversary beach walk.'

'Fair enough,' I smile. 'Time for a story before bed.'

Once there was a man who didn't want to die.

He left his family at home and set out on a journey to discover a country where death did not exist. Whenever he crossed a border, he strode up to a citizen and said to them, briskly: 'Do people die here? Do you bury them in the ground?' And when the answer came back: 'Of course!' he walked away from them, quickly, marching to another country where, when he got there, he'd ask the same thing.

Then eventually, one day, when the man was much older, he discovered a strange place, which wasn't on his map.

'Hello,' he said, to the first woman he saw. 'Do people die in this country? Do you bury them in the ground?'

'What's "die"?' the woman asked.

And the man's face brightened. 'It's normally what happens at the end of someone's life.'

'People's lives don't end here,' the woman said, looking puzzled. 'There just comes a point when they hear a strange voice, and they feel compelled to follow it. They pack their bags and leave and, for some reason, don't come back.'

The man jumped for joy. He bought a house for his family, and wrote a letter to them, asking them to come and find him in this new, exciting place. He hadn't seen them for years, and had missed out on most of their lives. But, he figured, if no one died in this strange place, then they had lots of time to make that right.

They lived happily together, and many years went by.

Then, one day, the man's wife sat up straight at the kitchen table.

'Can you hear that?' she asked.

'Hear what?' asked the man.

'It sounds like my father.' She stood, her chair clattering to the floor. 'It's my father's voice, and he's calling me. He wants me to come and find him. Where do you think it is that he is calling from?'

The man's blood ran cold, as he realised Death had cheated him.

He hurried to the front door and bolted it shut.

He locked all the windows and smashed his wife's phone.

'Listen to me,' he said. 'This voice is a trick. You must not follow it. Just pretend it's not there.'

But his wife could not pretend. The voice was so loud, and her body felt so small. She cried and tore her hair. She searched for tools to break the locks. She kicked the door until her feet bled. Then she screamed and clutched her skull.

Soon, the man simply couldn't take it any longer, for his wife was threatening to jump from the roof of their house.

'OK,' he said, his hands shaking. 'But please just remember. Once you've found your father, you must come back home to me.'

He unlocked their front door, and his wife ran out into the evening.

He watched her pelt across the fields . . . and she never came back.

'Did she call for him, though?' Mr Henderson interrupts. 'Later, years later, when it was his turn to die?'

'Yes,' I smile quickly. 'She came back to get him. She clasped him by the hand and whisked him away.'

Both Trevor and Mr Henderson lie back with a sigh.

I tuck them in, hammer in the nails, and sing a lullaby.

Once I hear Mr Henderson breathing deeply, I open the bottle of rose-water and spray it through the air vent. I select different sounds of the sea, and put them on a loop. Then I filter these into his coffin through a secret speaker on the side.

'There are different sorts of magic,' Aunt Libby always tells me. 'There is hope, and there is suggestion, and there is listening to the hurt.'

I hear footsteps running along the corridor outside.

Mr Henderson snores.

Yawning, I make my way out of the room. Aunt Libby's upstairs, singing badly in the shower. I find Cerberus in the kitchen, his tail between his legs.

'What's wrong?' I beckon, but he refuses to come closer. 'Are you sulking because you've been left here all alone?'

He whimpers and moans, and then hides under the table.

'Have it your way,' I tut, turning towards the window, and I jump so violently the rose-water smashes on the floor.

Outside, in the dark, just inches from the house, are the red lights from the woods. But they're moving on their own. They wave like a scarf. They flicker and they glimmer. They bang against the window, frantic on the wind.

'Ankaa!' Aunt Libby calls. 'Did you leave the front door open?'

Then there are footsteps close behind me, and Cerberus is howling, and all I can smell is roses on the air.

Sea Devils

We spent that summer killing crabs.

'They ain't natural,' Tabs said, eycing their sideways walk through her grandfather's monocle. 'They're bad, see. They gotta go.'

I took Tabs seriously. It was the way she chewed on old fishing nets, flossing all day so she'd have a smile fit to be in the movies with. I reckoned she could make it, see. Her hair was this black slate, a cloak for vampire fights, and the only reason she hadn't sailed off to Hollywood yct was 'cause she was in love with Wayne Cross from school. He'd morphed his parents' tractor into some kind of motorbike. Tabs said he was like a foreigner.

We went fishing for crabs twice a week and killed like we were warriors. Rolled our trousers up, peeled our socks off and tucked 'em into our knickers. We caught the monsters, standing barefoot, hauling in our nets.

The seaweed got stuck under our toenails and turned 'em violent green.

'Wash 'em off – you'll get gangrene,' Tabs said, tipping

a whole load of crabs into a veggie box she'd dragged along the sand.

I stared at my feet. 'Will it make me a mermaid?'

'It'll give you two left feet,' she grinned, ripping an arm off the nearest crab. 'And then you'll have to serve drinks at the church fayre instead of dancin'.'

'I ain't good at dancin'.'

'Neither are these,' she said, kicking the box. 'Drunken devils, all of 'em.'

The crabs were bad 'cause they were the devil in disguise. Crabs, we'd been told by Gracie's older sister, was a disease you got when you were bad with a boy.

'They're blue in the sea, and red when they're cooked,' Tabs said. 'They're red when they're shown the fires of hell, see. That's their true colours. Crabs are the devil and the devil wants us to rant and rave. He wants us to take off our knickers and lay down with him on the cliff tops. He wants us to throw out our souls like stinkin' rubbish. And then we can't ever go to Hollywood.'

I nodded at this logic.

'If you're unclean with a boy, you have to drink the blood of a cat and pray for forgiveness.'

'Ain't it a bad thing, cat killin'?' I asked. I was worried for our cat, Feda, who was out half the night.

'Not in the eyes of the Lord,' she said, angel-like. 'Not when the blood's for cleaning souls.'

We crossed ourselves hard and looked to the sky.

'One day, there'll be a path, or a ship or summat,' Tabs said, skipping along the rocks. 'And then w'can run away, see.' She slipped on some seaweed then and her blood was the colour of burnt anemone. She cursed and threw her face into the water, yelling down at whatever was in there. The waves swallowed the sound and changed it into bubbles. Tabs came up spitting, choking, yelling her rehearsed words of war.

It's hard work, see, chasing devils out of our kingdom.

Me and Ma live two streets away from Tabs. We live in a house with Frank. He ain't my dad though, see, my dad was a pirate – he was probably famous and everything but Ma doesn't like to talk about it. He was killed by a sea-devil what swallowed his ship. Frank ain't nothing like a pirate; he's a wuss. He collects bugs – all kinds of 'em. He traps 'em, gasses 'em and carries 'em around in a mauve leather suitcase. Once, he whipped out a giant silk moth and said it reminded him of Ma.

He spends most of his time in our greenhouse, polishing the windows.

I reckon if our house was flooded by a sea-devil, Frank's suitcase would swell up and pop open and all the paralysed bodies of the butterflies and luna moths and woolly bear caterpillars would drown, 'cause they don't know how to swim good. I wouldn't though, see. I'm the best swimmer on our street. Ma says you've got to know how to swim good when you live on an island.

She says an island's just an atom, waving at the sky.

'Let's play pretend,' Tabs said.

Those days never ended well.

That time she reckoned we should play Houdini and strap ourselves to chairs – throw ourselves out from the rocks and flap our legs like dancers. Cross ourselves and whisper prayers and hope we didn't drown.

'Like them witch trials,' she said, peeling a starfish off her bucket.

'We ain't witches, are we? 'Cause witches ain't good people.'

'Witches is devilry,' Tabs spat. 'They get to wear nice clothes in movies, but in real life they're evil-bad. Movies is where people can act out the Bad Stuff, 'cause movies is only pretend.'

Then she made me strap her to a dining-room chair and throw her out to sea.

The month Wayne Cross got a video camera, Tabs did a lot of Bad Stuff. She'd go visit him in the afternoons when she was supposed to be egg-collecting. She met him in the barn beside his parents' cattle shed; told me she was halfway to Hollywood, and I was left to catch crabs on my very own, scraping all my hair up high so as to watch the tide better. Sometimes it can sneak up on you quick, see, like it's stealin' the crabs back into its mouth.

I broke the crabs apart from their bodies so the devil couldn't reincarnate. Then I lit a fire in the back of the cave with a match I'd stolen from church. God wouldn't mind, but the vicar might, so I didn't tell him. Crabs don't really go up in flames 'cause the devil is resisting. They go red and then – later – they go black, like the colour of their souls. They smell bad, too, like fingers on fire.

It was a long summer, crab-killin'. My skin got red and my hair went wild. Some days Tabs came, and some days she didn't. When she did, she had a fire in her eyes, like she'd danced all night. She'd stopped chewing nets and started chewing tobacco. One day she said she felt butter-flies growing fast in the centre of her belly and I threw the net over her head, joking-like. She rolled around in the dirt and said she was like buried treasure. Then she laughed so hard I thought she might explode.

Mostly, she lay on her back and let me do all the work. She talked about how she was starring in films that were selling in a shop far, far away. The only shop I know of is Martha Graham's greengrocer's, but I kept quiet 'cause sometimes Tabs likes to play pretend. She's full of stories, she is. A tank full up to the brim with hundreds of words that all mean different things.

'My cat's missing,' I told her. 'You haven't seen Feda, have you?'

She stared straight past me and pretended not to hear.

'I'm saving up,' Tabs said. 'One day, I'll swim out into nowhere, and then I'll be everywhere, see.'

I nodded, as though I knew what she meant. But all I could think of was dark holes and nothingness. Like when you close your eyes tight and see strange fireworks there.

Feda had been missing for three days when I found him. It was late at night and he'd bled out from the neck. His fur was all matted, and his body was swollen. I found him floating in a rock pool down by the bay. I tried to hunt for his cat-soul but I didn't know what it would look like. So I just patted his broken head and looked out to sea.

One day, I thought, a huge wave is going to come. And I'm the only one who knows how to swim.

I could hear her then, Tabs, up on the cliffs. The whirr of a video camera. Grunts in the dark. Wayne Cross angling her bones to the light. Tabs burying her way to Hollywood, smiling all the way.

Human Satellites

To the north-east of our galaxy, there's a planet called The Hours.

Time migrates there from other superclusters; it's where atoms flee to retire.

The Hours is composed of soundbites from across the universe. Snippets of time and space pulled in by some foreign gravity that lines them up like jigsaws.

Like moving conveyor belts.

Like films.

When astronauts fly past it, their very atoms stir.

The surface of The Hours is obscured by the half-lives and faces contained in the snippets of time and space that live there. Those flickering stories with no stars to power them. The half lit half-light.

They take turns showing themselves, advertising life. Creatures we can barely imagine and oceans that aren't made out of water.

Microbes dancing microscopically.

The planet folds in on itself and expands, kicking at its skin like a baby bump.

Scientists pore at the surface, taking samples to try and carbon date each square inch. Inexplicably, some pieces are from the future and so are yet to exist.

Physicists fumble at these half-empty spaces that are not really empty, cupping the future, terrified that they will see into its murky depths and witness something that they do not want to witness. And terrified that they might accidentally alter the course of history.

They hear butterfly whispers and disembodied voices calling to them in their sleep.

But what is sleep? people start to ask. And there is silence.

Back on Earth, there are banners, protests, wars to STOP EXAMINING THE HOURS. To leave the planet alone in the cosmos.

Some things, a news reporter says, shivering outside the White House, *some things are meant to be left in the dark.*

Christian sects declare that The Hours is God. Hunched up and morphing in the depths of Dark Matter.

Some say we should run away. Some say we should go forth.

Some start a petition to bring the planet's water home to sell as holy water. To bathe in God. To consume him.

The Pope launches an online campaign to send priests into space.

A Seer says he has visited The Hours in a previous life.

The non-religious start converting at an alarming rate.

Celebrities talk about visiting The Hours. They bid to buy land there. The air is breathable in some parts, some of the time, some scientists say.

There are jokes about Time Share, about Moving Into the Future.

Nuclear bunkers are discounted everywhere.

Astrologers band together to form a cult worshipping The Hours. They hold replicas in their hands, strange space-crystal balls that they bought online from an anonymous seller.

Some say The Hours is the Internet in physical form.

They say that it's a virus and that all of us are infected.

Google's top one hundred questions no longer relate to anything found on Earth. Anthropologists say we have moved beyond that now.

Some say The Hours is a government conspiracy to distract everyone from 'problems at home.' Journalists start asking what the word *home* means and where its boundaries lie, while governments bicker over who The Hours rightfully belongs to, lining up flags.

PhD students sign up to circumnavigate The Hours: to become human satellites, so that over one thousand television stations and millions of YouTube channels can constantly stream the surface.

#TheHours.

Everyone watches.

Companies flock to advertise on the side of starlit space-suits.

What does it want, though? a news reporter asks, huddled under an umbrella. *Has anyone thought to ask it? Can it understand us at all?*

Statistics show that the world's population is finding it difficult to sleep. People giggle-cry into their coffee. Medication costs skyrocket.

Anti-gravity yoga classes are suddenly all the rage.

T-shirts are being printed by the millions: *IT'S WRITTEN IN THE STARS.*

The Hours Causes Cancer! headlines shout.

The Hours: Possible Alien Life Forms To Invade?

Some say The Hours is an optical illusion or perhaps a reality TV show.

Some say it's a hoax.

Scientists sigh and shrug their shoulders, theories running round and round in orbits.

Some say The Hours is us in the future – an us that wants revenge.

Others say it's an omen – that it's the devil in disguise.

A black hole that's going to open its mouth and swallow us down whole.

Bright White Hearts

'The sky is falling!' I cried. 'It's falling fast!'

'Where?'

'It's falling into the ocean.'

And everyone watched as the sun sank into the sea, and the moon laughed from the clouds, and the people cried until salt water came up to their chins.

'The water wants our words,' they said. 'It can't have them!'

The alphabet ran rivers from their mouths.

'Don't fight it,' I said, swimming between them. 'In a past life, we were jellyfish. And just look at us now.

'You'll get used to it. Learn to float.

Lie back.

Take steadying breaths.

It's all going to be OK.'

Welcome to the aquarium.

I work here on Saturdays.

Here, we like the colour blue.

Some scientists argue that ancient civilisations couldn't see the colour blue because they didn't have a name for it.

Then the Egyptians started to paint the sky on everything. Their blue had a luminescence, a halo. Lighting up under microscopes like fragments of outer space.

Let's talk about cosmic dust. As much as 40,000 tonnes of it rains down on us every year. Some of it falls from planetary rings, which would explain why I feel like I'm standing inside an orb most of the time. I stretch out my arms and touch all of the things I cannot see.

Other people can't see them, either. They ignore my galactic rules and invade my personal space.

In the sea, instead of cosmic dust, there is something called marine snow. White flakes of dead fish that trickle down into the darkness to feed those below.

Like standing out in the rain and sticking out your tongue.

The dead skin of stars and the dead skin of Pisces.

Hello, Aquarius.

We are all made of starfish.

Sometimes, people look at me strangely. They are very wary about touching the headsets I hand out to them at work, in case I've contaminated them somehow.

I was born with my fingers joined together, but now they are separated. Scars scatter my hands like nets, caught by science. I'm missing some of them, too.

Sometimes I tell people sharks ate my fingers, just to see the looks on their faces.

I was given a written warning at work for saying that, in case customers thought that we'd broken health and safety rules.

'Welcome to the aquarium, where sharks will *not* eat your fingers.'

My toes are joined together, too.

I pass a headset to a woman and her two children, and she holds it, gingerly, at arm's length, glaring. The headphones pincered between two fingers. Like a crab.

Just keep swimming.

Sometimes people get annoyed because David Attenborough doesn't narrate the audio tour.

They ask me for a refund.

'I'm afraid we have a no refund policy.'

Sometimes people ask me if we have freed the angry orcas yet, and I have to say:

'We are not affiliated with SeaWorld.'

But they don't believe the girl with missing fingers.

I suppose that's fair enough, considering my lie about the shark.

Sharks are fascinating creatures.

The goblin shark lives near the bottom of the ocean. Like the narwhal, he is a unicorn of the deep. One of the many unicorns we dismiss as 'not real' because he doesn't shine with the beauty we imagine imperative. Instead, scientists call him a living fossil; they're not sure why evolution has let him pass. He is death, swimming out of sight. A fairy tale, his skin crinkled and pink, as though just born. Sometimes, fishermen accidentally haul him to the surface and hurriedly throw him back. No one wants an ugly history, dying, on the deck of their ship.

In the sea, we lose our colour, the deeper we go. Until skin becomes transparent and not-quite-there. Ghost shrimp, and glass squids. Vases of the deep: organs blooming in fluorescent lights, and bodies floating like brains. If the sea is the sky, these are our aliens.

I like to sit at the bottom of the bath to see if I lose my colour, too.

When I am half asleep, I like to talk to myself as though I am underwater.

When it rains, I stand outside and wait for my scales to show.

Crocodile icefish live in the depths of Antarctica. Swimming stars with transparent blood. They have no haemoglobin or myoglobin so, beneath their jelly skin, you can see them pulsing. Musical fish, beating, with bright, white hearts.

We don't have many exotic fish at the aquarium. But we do have mantis shrimp. You might not think that's exciting, but it is. They are the size of a finger, and have the most complex vision of any living creature we know. Humans have just three colour cones. We see blue and red and green and all of the colours those can blend. Butterflies have five colour cones, and their rainbows are brighter. The mantis shrimp has *sixteen*, and we have no idea what their world looks like. Colours that don't have names slinking across the waves.

The mantis shrimp can also eat octopuses, and even break aquarium walls.

We keep a very close eye on them.

Scientists have invented an injection for colour. It hasn't been tried on humans yet, only monkeys. A cure for colour-blindness.

My dad is colour-blind.

Scientists also believe that some women have four colour cones. That their skies look different. That their blues are more varied. Colour enthusiasts chase these women all over the world. We have an obsession with things just out of our reach.

I'm sure that gravity has a colour.

I like to think that colours were created by children, somewhere. Breathing names out into the dark.

When I was small, I saw a documentary where a blind man regained his sight, and he looked down at his black jeans and said to his wife: 'You told me these were green. Green's my favourite colour.'

And she laughed and said, 'I wasn't going to let you wear green jeans. And, anyway, I thought you'd never know.'

He'd had those jeans for six years.

Did you know there is a shade of blue called Space Cadet?

And did you know that, in China, shades of blue are called *shallow* or *deep*, not *light* or *dark*?

Our aquarium uniforms are orange. They are not very flattering.

My favourite tank is the water tunnel. A huge pool full of squid and stingray. The public walk beneath it, surrounded by water above and around, so they can imagine that they are at the bottom of the sea. I watch children run from one end to the other, holding their breath the whole way. Giggling nervously, tapping the glass to make sure that it's strong enough.

'This is like a submarine!' a young boy cries, colliding with my leg.

He doesn't apologise.

When *Finding Nemo* was released we had our busiest weekend ever.

'Excuse me,' his mother says. 'Are any of these fish for sale?'

Transparent zebra fish are used for cancer research. Scientists like them because they can see their insides without ever having to cut them open. They plant stories inside and wait for the end.

Once upon a time, I jumped into a story.

I won my first goldfish at the summer fayre in a child's version of beer pong. I remember my parents, outraged, shouting at the headmistress. Stuff about promising children animals as a con from the local pet shop. A free goldfish so long as you buy the expensive tank to put it in. Some redundant bridges. Food. And cleaning equipment, too.

'We should just flush it down the loo,' my dad said, holding the plastic bubble of water.

A mini world.

A lost soul stuck in the centre.

And off we went to the pet shop, my father swearing profusely, and my mother telling him to *please be quiet, otherwise people might hear.*

Things have changed a lot since then. For instance, in America, now you can buy GloFish® (Experience the Glo!®) – genetically modified fish that glow in the dark.

They come in red, green, orange, blue, pink and purple. They were originally bred to help detect pollution.

Have you seen those people taking a break from their shopping, who pay to have fish nibble at the dead skin on their feet?

They laugh while it's happening. *Garra rufa*. Toothless little carps from Turkey.

Put on a show!

Smile for the people!

Now, now. Eat them nicely.

In ancient Egypt and Rome, military commanders painted their nails to match their lips before they charged into battle.

Perhaps if I dipped my feet into the tank, they would eat away at the skin between my toes. Gnaw at my rough edges and let me emerge a princess. A water nymph.

Because princess is beauty.

So they tell me.

Every single day.

Did you know that we used to think that princes and princesses had blue blood?

In Inuit mythology, a giant called Sedna was unhappy with the men her father wanted her to marry, so she married a dog instead. Her father threw her into the sea in outrage and, when she tried to cling to the side of the ship, he cut off her fingers with an axe. Her fingers fell into the sea and took on a life of their own. They became the seals and whales of the ocean, and Sedna grew up to be a goddess of the deep.

I like origin stories.

When I grow up, I want to be . . .

The vampire squid that lives at the bottom of the ocean. It turns itself inside out and morphs its organs into traffic lights. It has three hearts because it has learned that one is not enough.

At the weekend, we do something we probably shouldn't.

Something we *definitely* shouldn't.

Once all of the children have gone home, we lock the front doors, change our clothes and hold our breath.

We section off the big tank, and filter the floodlights. Mr Farani says it's the only way we can make ends meet. Things have been quiet recently. But not on Saturday nights.

We can't talk about it loudly. It's passed in whispers through the streets. We dim the bulbs and shine subtly. Like GloFish®. Like plankton.

Dinoflagellates are a sort of plankton and they are biolu-minescent. They have two tails, and create a red tide when all of them come together. This is called an algal bloom. A red sea.

This is not the same as The Red Sea. That's Al Bahr al-Ahmar and is something else entirely. It touches nine different countries and has twenty-five islands, and seventeen major shipwrecks that it's swallowed down whole.

There are lots of plankton there, too, though.

People think that plankton are entirely insignificant, but together they weigh more than all the other living things.

The Dead Sea is different. It spits up black asphalt. The Egyptians trekked far to get their mummification balm there. Some say it's haunted by fish spirits killed by high salinity. Occasionally, things are born there, after heavy rain. Propelling themselves to life before the salt levels rise.

The Dead Sea is a brilliant turquoise. A floating machine. But, in the wet winter of 1980, it bled deep crimson. An explosion of red algae, dancing in the rain.

We all come from the sea, really.

Glistening humans, feeling for gills.

Seventy per cent water.

Shimmering foetuses.

We are clumsy on land.

We are clumsy in water.

And don't get me started on what we're like in the air.

We're an embarrassment.

We are so insignificant.

Did you hear about that hotel in Florida where you can get married underwater? Wedding vows as bubbles and chlorine shooting up your nose. And, did you know, in Argentina, a baby dolphin was washed up on the shore? Sunbathers passed it around the beach, taking selfies. Hugging it close.

Put on a show!

Smile for the people!

And the dolphin died, right there, surrounded by humans. Far too over-exposed.

We all come from the sea. Just some of us more than others.

Once upon a time, a girl jumped into the sea.

There wasn't anyone around, so she might have made no noise.

If a girl falls down.

If

a

girl

falls

down.

Does anyone hear it?

It was in the days before the sea and sky had been sliced in two, so no one knew if she jumped up or down, or in or around, but she jumped well.

And the air and the sky slipped through her fingers.

And the limpets were stars that clung to her knees.

And the sun bubbled like a blowhole in a far-off galaxy.

This girl was from an island that no one had left before.

And she was strange. And she was different.

And everyone was scared of the way she talked, which happened to be not at all.

They called her many things, and they named her many times.

And, then, when they were done, they told her to swim.

Swim into the nameless colour, and tell them what was there.

Whether the world was flat, and if water dragons were fierce.

And if a space whale had once fallen into the sea in a shower of liquid stars.

They packed her a lunch, and watched her go.

And prayed she'd never come back.

So, off she went

    a

    girl

pushed

into

the

sea.

She swam until her skin turned blue.

She swam until her feet were webbed.

She swam until she saw a light, lurking, far beneath her feet.

A light that buzzed and hummed and sang within a gigantic shell of bone.

The girl tapped it once. She tapped it twice.

And on the third tap it opened, like a broken jaw.

When the bubbles cleared, she saw a cushion there.

On it were pearls.

No, not pearls.

Teeth.

Rows and rows of strangers' teeth.

The teeth flew out of her hands.

And clung to her neck.

And locked themselves into place there.

And then she could see all the colours.

And then she could hear all the stories.

And then she knew that she was not alone.

*

Welcome to our night-time aquarium.

We've turned the underwater tunnel into a cocktail bar and by ten p.m. it's packed with those clamouring to see. Men below, looking up, and men above, looking down. We have glasses with umbrellas and Mr Farani serves grilled shrimp. The men in the tunnel are banging the glass.

Put on a show!
  Smile for the people!

Let's talk about butterfly stroke. I am not very good at butterfly stroke.

Are you? Is anyone?

Sea butterflies are pteropods and they are nearly invisible to the naked eye. They have feet that they use as wings to swim through the ocean.

Some pteropods are called sea angels.
  Sea angels.

The love of my life is called Melissa Singh.
  Melissa Singh is our underwater ballerina.
  Our in-house evening mermaid.

My job is to hold Melissa's inhaler. I help her get into her costume, too. I have to sew the sequins back on if any of them fall off. They fall off quite a lot. It's a very important job. It is also very difficult to walk with a tail. Melissa makes it look easy, in her cheap bubblegum bra. She poses for the punters and they throw silver in the water; they shower her with stars and she pretends not to mind. Then she curls her pink tail (this shade of pink is called *flamingo*), shoves her hair behind her ears and dives into the tank.

I hold my breath in solidarity. My lungs a burning coral.

The world record is twenty minutes and, after that, you disappear.

In Eastern Europe, some mermaids are called *rusalky*. They are dangerous, demonic creatures who love to dance and drown.

Russia has a proverb: 'Not everything is a mermaid that dives into the sea.'

Melissa has a scar.

A big one, on her right leg. It runs all the way from her ankle to just inside her thigh. It's a glistening constellation. It matches my hands. She caught me looking one time, and gave me a look of defiance. Perhaps we are the same, I thought. Perhaps we come from a similar home.

I've spent all this week reading up on Sirenomelia. Babies born into this world swimming, with their legs fused together. The likelihood of this happening is the same as conjoined twins.

We are all born with our shadows underwater.
    Tiktaalik are the first fish that scientists think could crawl.

Melissa surfaces, gasping, as though unused to air.
    Lungfish are ancient species that used to be everywhere.
    Now you can only find them in the Southern Hemisphere.

Melissa floats, symmetrical.
    Sequins falling from her tail.
    She is our only northern lungfish.

I hold tightly to her inhaler, and recite species off by heart.
    Plankton have such ridiculous names:

The Spiral Curvydisc
The Potbellied Gravyboat
The Necklaced Ladderwedge

Until the 1880s, anyone born with a deformity was medically called a monster.
    What is the etymology of etymology?
    Google says it comes from *etmos*, meaning *true*.
    How hilarious our world is.

Melissa's hair billows like seaweed.

In Siberia, *rusalky* look like yetis.

In West Africa there are water gods with snake bodies called Nommo.

In the 1780s, Charles Byrne was born in Ireland, and it was rumoured he grew up to be eight feet tall. People called him The Irish Giant, and he travelled across to London. He'd heard he could make money in the city's bizarre sideshows.

Scientists loved Charles Byrne. They said he'd grown so tall because he'd been conceived on top of a haystack.

They said Madam Howard was born with a mane because her father was eaten by a lion.

They said the Lobster Boy had a mother who'd craved shellfish when he was in her womb.

The Irish Giant drank himself to death at the age of twenty-two and, not wanting scientists to dissect him, he paid a fisherman in Bristol to bury him at sea.

The fisherman faked a water funeral and sold his body back to science.

He's still on display, in London, for anyone to see.

It is uncomfortably hot in here.

I watch the Raja Binoculata float by. A flat fish, skimming, with the face of a startled human.

Melissa told me she fell off her bike when she was little. She said the doctors had to sew her back together again. She said she's never even heard of medical mermaids, and now everyone around us is taking her photograph.

Melissa means bee, and Singh means lion-blooded.
 Sea lion.
 Sea angel.
 Brittle sea star.

Did you know a starfish is an asteroid?
 And some brittle stars have six tentacles?
 And some starfish can regrow their arms but, really, they'd rather not?

I squeeze Melissa's inhaler in the palm of my hand, and then suddenly realise I'm still holding my breath.

We all come from the sea.
 Blurry and ancient. Slowly evolving.

We are photographs, developing.
 I wonder, can you see my heart?

Author's Note

The history of fairy tales is a subject I'm forever fascinated by. Twisted stories that have weaved their way through the centuries, morphing and breeding under the spell of so many different storytellers. If you'd like to know more about the history of these beasts (for, really, what is a fairy tale if not alive?) then head over to my YouTube channel, where you can find a whole series on this very topic: youtube.com/jenvcampbell.

I talk about a lot of other book-related things there, too, and as a queer woman with a deformity, representation in the media is also a subject close to my heart, so you can find videos about that, as well.

Acknowledgements

Thank you to my editor, Lisa. Here's to fairy tales, the weirder the better.

Thank you to my agent, Charlie, for not shouting when I said I was writing short stories instead of a novel.

Thank you to the team at Two Roads.

Thank you to booksellers, librarians and festival organisers.

Thank you to my writerly pals for your words of encouragement.

Thank you to those of you who watch my YouTube channel.

Thank you to my friends for listening to me talk about this book. A lot.

Thank you to my family.

Thank you to Miles.

And thank you.

You.

Whoever you are, wherever you are, reading this book. x

A Note on the Text

'Margaret and Mary and the End of the World' contains a few lines from the poems of Christina Rossetti.

'Pebbles' was first published in *New Welsh Review*.

About the Author

Jen Campbell is an award-winning poet and short story writer. She grew up in a small village by the sea in the north-east of England, and is the *Sunday Times* bestselling author of the *Weird Things Customers Say in Bookshops* series and *The Bookshop Book*. She won an Eric Gregory Award in 2016, her poetry collection *The Hungry Ghost Festival* is published by The Rialto, and her children's book *Franklin's Flying Bookshop* is published by Thames & Hudson. Jen worked as a bookseller for ten years and talks about all things books over at youtube.com/jenvcampbell. She currently lives in London.